Happy Birth...
from Grandma Haddin
We to and may you
have many of them
Da
September 2nd 1953

Blue Smoke

by the same author

SILVER BIRCH

MIDNIGHT MOON

GOLDEN SOVEREIGN

RED EMBERS

HARLEQUIN HULLABALOO

COPPER KHAN

DARK SUNSHINE

Blue Smoke

DOROTHY LYONS

Illustrated by Wesley Dennis

HARCOURT, BRACE AND COMPANY, NEW YORK

LIBRARY OF CONGRESS CATALOG CARD NUMBER: 53-7867

PRINTED IN THE UNITED STATES OF AMERICA

Table of Contents

1. KING IN DISGUISE   3

2. BEYOND PRICE   14

3. KID BROKE AND LADY GENTLE   26

4. NOMAD NO LONGER   36

5. B PLUS A EQUALS X   45

6. KILLER?   58

7. WARD OF THE COURT   69

8. SKELETON IN THE CLOSET   82

9. BLUE SUNDAY   92

10. FRESH START   105

11. "NO NEXT TIME"   115

12. FINGER EXERCISES   126

13. BLACK AND BLUE   137

14. FULL SCALE HIDE-AND-SEEK   147

15. COWBOY FROM LOS ANGELES   159

16. FIRST STEP   169

17. CHEST X-RAY   178

18. VIVA LA FIESTA!   188

19. I CHALLENGE   200

20. A LOSING VICTORY   211

21. WAKING NIGHTMARE   223

22. FOR KEEPS   232

Blue Smoke

·1·

King in Disguise

Andrea Bard of the Bar D Guest Ranch turned to face her younger brother who banged through the screen door to slump in a chair on the spacious veranda beside her. His freckles and sunburned butch cut added up to but one thing, small boy.

"Penny for your thoughts, Andy."

"Knowing you're one of the penniless Bards, I'll have to see the color of your money first," she demurred.

He drew a fist from his pocket, slowly opening it to show his empty palm.

"Just as I thought. Well, that's about all my thoughts were worth. I was wondering what had happened to that horde of dudes we worked so madly to get ready for. I've been sitting here pretending I was a dude but I can't find anything wrong with the place whichever way I look."

Her arms spread out to include the tree-dotted meadow where the ranch buildings and corrals clustered beside a busy little stream that fizzed along its rocky bed, the valley that opened up to the right and the left between two mountainous ridges. The warm California sun smiled down on the scene proudly, taking all the credit to itself for lush grass, bright flowers, and fresh green trees where birds trilled happily, completely ignoring the life-sustaining winter rains.

"Ah-h, don't worry, Andy. It's early yet. The May magazines with our ads haven't been out more than a week or two yet."

"Yes, Jump, but seems as if we'd have heard from an eager beaver or two who wanted to get in ahead of the rush."

"I wish all of you would stop calling me that. My name is Jack."

"I should think you'd have given up by this time. You've been called that for twelve years, since you were a baby when you *were* a Jumping Jack. You ought to like it. Think of all the Jacks and Jims and Bills."

The screen door banged again and a younger girl, her legs seemingly as long and thin as her two braids, came out with a piece of bread and honey in each hand. Jump reached out and took the extra piece which she relinquished as if she knew it was not really hers.

"Thanks, Val. How'd you know I was hungry?"

" 'Cause you always are," Val answered matter-of-factly. "Let's go for a horseback ride, Andy."

"Yeah, gotta keep those horses ridden down so's they won't give the dudes any trouble," Jump leered.

"I don't feel like riding. You two go along. And stop at the mailbox on your way home."

Once more alone Andrea Bard resumed her gloomy review of the past months' feverish activity: her mother's decision to bolster their income from a sluggish beef market by adding dudes as a by-product, their energetic cleaning and remodeling to adapt their comfortable old ranchhouse to paying guests, the modest advertisements inserted in horse and travel magazines and, finally, the large areas of unoccupied space. She tried to recapture the illusion that she was a dude.

She might well have been one. Her high-heeled boots, blue jeans and bright plaid shirt had the worn look that part-time westerners strive for. There was an alert, ready-for-anything air about her from her thick, short bob of what she called "hair-colored" hair, tanned face that framed her gray eyes and a mouth that even immobile seemed to smile.

Judged against a height-weight table for fifteen-year-olds she would have been taller and slimmer than average but she carried her extra inches proudly, perhaps because her mother had told her she was tall and straight like her father instead of saying, "Do stand up straight!"

"Not out riding on the first Saturday in May?" Mrs. Bard herself came up on the porch and dropped into the swing.

"No. I know we have to have gentle horses for dudes, Muz, but they're just too tame to be much fun. I sure wish I could earn enough money for a horse of my own, but out in the country like we are there's just no chance."

"I'd buy you one myself if I could, dear. I've leaned on you so much since your father died, especially last year when my health was poor, you've had to grow up too fast. Satisfying your one burning desire would be little enough reward."

"You haven't *leaned* on me, Muz. We've just talked things over together."

"That's what I mean. That's what puts an old head on young shoulders. Perhaps next year we can manage it—if the dude business ever picks up."

In repose Mrs. Bard's face had a sad, gentle quality that fled when her mouth turned up in a smile and a twinkle brightened her eyes. For the first time Andy noticed a thread of gray here and there in the long hair coiled neatly at the back.

"Don't you worry, Muz. Those old dudes are sure to come any day now—any minute." The girl reversed herself and was determinedly hopeful. "Even if they don't, we've been getting along all right."

"True, but we'd get along better if we had all the rooms full. We've spent a lot of money fixing up for them, too. If only your father—"

Her voice trailed off into silence but Andy knew her mother was thinking of the reckless driver, the head-on crash six years before that had thrust head-of-the-family responsibilities on Mrs. Bard. Andy remembered her father vividly but in snatches, strong arms and a hearty voice that often boiled over into laughter, or punishment, swift and sure but just, when she had gotten out of line.

"You've done all right, Muz. Dad himself couldn't have done any better running the place than you have. We're lucky to have as good a foreman as Luis, too. It's a stroke of luck that he was born on this ranch and likes it so much he doesn't want to leave. He could get a dozen other good jobs here in the Santa Ynez Valley."

"I suppose every woman thinks her husband can work miracles. I'm sure John would have figured something out —and he wouldn't have had to have a pay-check every month," she finished wryly.

"Listen! Do you hear what I hear?" Andy exclaimed with excitement hard to control.

"I sure do. That was our bridge rumbling—someone's coming!"

Each had unconsciously inventoried the ranch's cars and knew they were all in. It might be a neighbor or anybody but—it might be business. They jumped up. They shouldn't be caught idle.

"Hurry down by the corrals and be doing something with the horses, Andy," Mrs. Bard whispered as if their guest could already hear them. "It'll be chilly tonight—I think I'll light the fire in the grate now."

Andy ran for the barn, pacing the car in her mind as it came nearer. She slowed her steps a little to listen better. When gears shifted for the last little hill she stopped completely. It must be a jalopy to shift on that grade. A battered nose poked into sight around the curve and before Andy had thoroughly appraised the old car she saw that it drew an even more battered horse trailer.

The girl motioned the driver, obscured by the windshield's reflection, toward their parking area but the car halted barely clear of the driveway. Andy waved the driver on but with no success, and when he made no move to get out she and her mother converged on the car. Mrs. Bard got there first.

"Would you—" she began.

"Ma'am, I saw your sign down by the gate. I feel a mite puny. Could I get a night's lodging for myself and my horse? I can pay," the old man said so defensively Mrs.

Bard would have known without seeing his outfit that money was not plentiful with him.

"Of course you can. Come right in and I'll get someone to look after your horse. Luis—" she called and as if at the clap of a genii's hands the foreman materialized.

Contrasted with Luis's rugged bulk the old man looked frail indeed and though his seamed face was tanned he looked so white and strained his eyes stood out like brown buttons on white cloth. Luis stretched out an arm to steady the visitor. But for that he would have wilted down beside the running board, his hands clutching his chest while he fought for breath.

With one motion the burly foreman scooped the old man up in his arms as easily as he would have a sack of grain, then looked to Mrs. Bard for orders.

"Put him to bed in the cottage, Luis. Andy, call the doctor."

"But, Muz," Andy faltered. "That's our best accommodation. Suppose—?"

"Can't be helped. He has to be where he'll have proper care—besides, we're not sure what he has. It looks like a heart attack but if it should be anything contagious, we can't have him in the big house."

Andy sprinted for the phone while her mother ran ahead of Luis to open the cottage door. By the time Andy returned with news that the doctor was on his way the patient was reviving. The sound of his labored breathing filled the room. Before his eyes opened one hand fumbled weakly with his shirt pocket.

"Just lie still, Pop. You'll be all right," Luis soothed. "Just take it easy," he said as he tried to calm the fluttering hand.

Fear shone from the old eyes, naked and eloquent as words, while his lips moved noiselessly, trying to tell them something. Mrs. Bard ran her fingers down in his pocket to draw out a brown medicine bottle.

" 'In case of a heart attack place one tablet under my tongue. Repeat in ten minutes if needed, and let me lie down," she read aloud.

Mrs. Bard hurriedly shook out a pill which she offered to the old man propped up in Luis's arms. The three watched breathlessly. Within a few minutes tenseness and fear left the brown eyes and the frail figure relaxed.

"There now, Pop, you're going to be all right. Take it easy," Luis murmured with a gentleness Andy had not known he possessed.

"The doctor'll be here in just a few minutes. Just close your eyes and rest," Mrs. Bard said, emphasizing it with a pat on the bony shoulder.

Pop's eyes spoke his thanks but he used what little strength he had for something dearer than himself.

"Look—after—Blue. He's—gen-gen—"

"We will, Pop," Andy put in. "He's gentle, eh?"

Again the brown eyes spoke for him as he sighed with a complete end of cares.

"Guess you won't need me for a while, Miz Bard. I'll go look after the horse," Luis said.

"Me, too, Muz. I'll be back in a jiff if you need me."

Outside, Luis decided to pull the car and trailer out of the way before unloading the horse.

"Old Blue and I'll see you at the barn," he said to Andy.

The foreman's Spanish heritage of olive skin and dark hair contrasted as strangely with the blue eyes of his Irish adventurer grandfather as did his first and last names, Luis

Riley. In one trait his mixed nationalities blended perfectly, however, the old Spanish don's matchless horsemanship mingling with and intensifying the Irishman's love of horse-flesh to produce a horseman who had few equals. Andy was always a willing second whenever he was around the horses and she too had become a top hand with a horse.

If possible, the trailer was more battered than the car but as it rolled toward the stables Andy decided it looked like a sturdy one. Its full canopy and side flaps hid all but a spot of grayish rump and dark tail of the blanketed horse within.

"He'll have to be quite a horse to live up to the rest of the outfit," she chuckled, "but I suppose the old boy loves him and that's what counts. Luis, maybe he's an ox, named for Paul Bunyan's old blue ox, Babe."

"Could be. I'm prepared for anything on four legs."

He loosened the bolts on the tailgate, rolled up a flap and, standing on the tire, talked in soft tones to the horse. After making certain that Blue was neither excited nor nervous, Luis undid the tie rope and ran it back over the tailgate.

"Now, Andy, you stand here to one side to hold the rope while I let the back down. Whoa, fellow. Easy does it."

The roan head in the shadowy interior turned and two wise eyes watched their progress. Standing well to one side where he wouldn't be caught if the horse rushed back, Luis lowered the gate softly but Blue stood like a gentleman.

"Gentle *and* mannerly, I'd say. He's waiting for an invitation. OK, old fellow, back. Back."

Andy tugged gently on the halter rope. Two oval bac]
hoofs were placed tentatively on the lowered ramp. At
second command the horse emerged slowly and deliberatel
until, with just his front hoofs on the ramp, he stopped t<
look around at his new surroundings.

Luis whistled. "If the rest of him lives up to that hea<
and neck, he's a beauty. Come clear out, boy. Let's ge
that sheet off and have a look at you."

When Blue obliged, Luis unbuckled the straps and peele<
off the ragged sheet.

"Jeepers, Luis, he's the pearl in the oyster," Andy
breathed. "Isn't he a dream?"

Andy understood at once the meaning of the horse'<
name. From his muzzle to his hocks he was roan, blue roan
with a perfect blending of white and black hairs and s<
shiny the sky itself lent more blue to him. Forelock, man<
and tail were also a blend of light and dark hairs but th<
latter predominated, giving him dark points to match hi<
slick, dark leggings.

Stripped of his ragged disguise Blue was every inch th<
king and a worthy descendant of those blocky littl<
sprinters that followed the nation's frontier from Virgini<
to the Pacific. Their short bursts of speed, whether chasing
a cow or racing on short courses hacked from the wilder
ness or staked out on dry western plains, eventually earne<
for them the name of quarter-mile or Quarter Horses.

"You're every inch a Quarter Horse, aren't you, Blue?"

Andy could hardly refrain from running her hands ove
him from the soft, short muzzle along his prominent cheek
bones to his tiny ears or across his brawny chest and shor

barrel to his rounded, sloping rump that set his legs well under him. Blue might well have served as a model for all Quarter Horses.

"Could you fault him anywhere, Luis?"

"Yes—I don't know where, but it's said that no horse is perfect. He's about as close to it as I'd ever hope to come though. Looks like he has been eating a lot better than his boss but there isn't an ounce of unnecessary fat on him."

"I'll take him in, Luis. What stall had he better have?"

"The first one, I guess, where we can keep an eye on him and it's built stronger than the others. But you'd better let me do it, Andy. After all, Blue is a stallion, so until we know him better we ought to treat him with respect."

"But Pop said he was gentle, and you couldn't find a better-mannered horse," the girl protested but she nevertheless stepped back while Luis led the horse into the barn.

"Gentle with his owner is one thing but gentle with total strangers might be entirely different."

Andy hung around as the newcomer was shut securely in the vacant stall, given a tub of water, an armful of hay. After a get-acquainted snuff around his stall, Blue settled down to his hay, yet he was too polite to ignore his guests, favoring them with his tranquil gaze and cocked ears so long as they stayed.

· 2 ·

Beyond Price

The doctor had arrived when Andy returned to Pop's cottage and she waited outside on the steps. It was not long before footsteps approached the door and Muz and the doctor came out.

"You did just the right thing, Mrs. Bard," he was saying, "and Pop Whoever-he-is ought to be able to be up in a day or two—until the next attack comes along. He was very lucky to have found a place like this when he needed it so desperately. Just see that he gets plenty of rest and eats sensibly."

"Can I go in and talk to him, Muz?" Andy asked after the doctor drove away. "He's probably wondering about Blue."

"Yes, you can, and what's more you can stay with him while I help Rosita with supper—it'll be late enough now."

Andy opened the door softly and tiptoed toward the bed until she saw Pop's eyes, sharper than they had been earlier, fixed on her. She smiled easily and sat down beside him.

"We've unloaded Blue and put him in a big box stall where he'll be all right and couldn't possibly hurt himself. We've watered and fed him too." She paused to make sure he understood her. The corners of the old man's mouth turned up in the faintest smile.

"He's sure a dandy. No wonder you take such good care of him."

Her enthusiasm overrode her sickroom manners while she chattered on about the horse. Glancing at the patient, she saw that his eyes were closed. She half jumped to her feet before she realized, noting the steady rise and fall of the bedclothes, that past the crisis and his concern over Blue, Pop was having a nap.

She wondered where he had slept the night before. Wherever it had been the old man had made the effort to shave that morning. Andy saw that his clothes, piled on a nearby chair, had been darned and mended until little of the original material remained, but they were as clean as her own.

It almost seemed like spying to search the worn face for its story, but it told her little enough. Thin it was and white beneath its tan. Contrasting it with the horse's rounded perfection brought a choke to Andy's throat, for she could guess that often Blue had had full rations when his owner had not.

Outside she heard Val and Jump cantering toward the house in full cry.

"Hey, whose car and trailer out there, Noah's?"

"Hush!" Mrs. Bard ordered. "Put your horses away and get washed up for supper. I'll tell you later."

Mrs. Bard brought Pop's tray before their own meal was on the table. He ate lightly but with relish.

"Take it easy now and one of us will be right back after we eat. If you want anything meanwhile, just ring this bell." She smiled.

All of them, including Luis, gathered in the big dining room where they bowed their heads while Mrs. Bard said grace. An instant after her "Amen" everyone spoke at once.

"What I can't understand," Andy puzzled, "is why anyone with such a valuable horse should be so hard up."

"I have an idea," Luis said, then deliberately took a big bite of meat to tease the others.

The youngsters squirmed with impatience while Luis carefully chewed his mouthful, extra carefully they thought, before he continued.

"The horse is wearing racing plates, so I suppose the old man followed the races and evidently Blue just wasn't fast enough. Many a racehorse owner has gone hungry to keep his horse in condition."

"But Blue is a Quarter Horse, not a Thoroughbred. Could he pick up enough money in those races to live on?" Andy questioned.

"If his horse comes in first often enough, he could. Several tracks have been running an extra race every day just for short horses, and there's a meet down south for nothing but Quarter Horses. Likely Pop was starting off on the summer race and rodeo circuit."

Mrs. Bard returned to the cottage after supper to check on their patient. Andy trailed along. Pop had improved rapidly and his eyes were bright, almost gay.

"It's good to see you looking so much better. You felt pretty bad there for a while, Mr.—Mr.—?"

"Reed, but just Pop suits me," he countered. "I don't reckon I can ever repay for yore bein' so neighborly. It meant—everythin' to me."

"I'm just glad we were here when you needed us. Is there anyone expecting you tonight? Would you like us to notify someone of your whereabouts so they won't worry?" Mrs. Bard asked.

"Nope, don't bother. No one's worryin' about me—'less it's Blue. There's jest him'n me. He's my family."

This gave Andy an opening into the conversation which she snatched.

"Blue is getting along fine too. I wanted to ask you if there's anything special you'd want us to do for him to-night. He has hay and water."

"Take care—not too much hay, miss. He needs his oats. There's a sack of 'em in the back of my car with a scoop. Give him three of 'em. Sorry to bother you folks so."

"It's no bother! I just love looking at him."

"Goodness! I'll say it's no bother for Andy," her mother exclaimed. "She's horse-happy and would live with them if I'd let her."

Andy left to look after Blue but poked her head back in the door.

"Hey, I forgot to ask. Do you leave that sheet on him at night?"

"Yep, 'tain't much good but I'd hate for him to take a chill. Seems like the littlest cold or cough can play the dickens with a hoss's wind."

Going into the barn for a pail to put the grain in, And
was greeted by a lonesome nicker from Blue. She wer
over to his stall.

"Hello, fellow. What's on your mind? Not food, you'v
hay there you haven't touched. Not water. You hav
plenty. Just a little attention maybe? Well, come over her
and I'll pet you a while."

Her hand was raised to slip through the bars when Luis
warning jangled in her head, "treat him with respect." Sh
drew her arm back and looked at him thoughtfully. H
eyes were wise and placid. His ears cocked forward cur
ously.

"You must be sweet-tempered, Blue, but Luis is righ
Any strange stallion should be handled with care. I'm sorr
to be so stand-offish, but maybe you'll accept your oats :
a promissory note for the loving you'll get later—if Po
doesn't take you away too soon."

The pang such a thought gave her surprised Andy. Wh
should she feel so bad at losing a horse she had never see
before that day? In looking at the beautiful stallion sh
had her answer. Physically he was everything that a hors
should be and in addition his personality attracted her ju
as she liked some people more than others. It would b
wrong to hope that Pop didn't get well very fast, but sh
could hope that something else would delay him.

"Hold everything, Blue. I'll be back in a flash."

She scooped the grain (clean, first quality oats, she noted
into the pail and hurried back to Blue's stall where sh
poured them into the grain box. He plunged his nose t
the bottom of the box but after this one monstrous mouth

ful he slowed down, keeping track of Andy's whereabouts as he ate.

Instead of physical caresses she stood beside his stall, showering him with verbal loving while her eyes feasted on every glorious inch of him. Anyone mounted on such perfection would feel the equal of kings. Andy sighed, wondering whether she would ever have the good fortune to own half as good a horse.

Her daydreaming had overlapped into night dreaming, she suddenly realized, as the shadowy corners grew larger and finally blended with each other in one large blanket of darkness. Blue was only another shadow to Andy who was about to leave when she remembered his sheet.

"Glory! What'll I do if Luis has gone to town for Saturday night?"

She sprinted for the bunkhouse where she saw a light in the foreman's window. She called him out to explain.

"I'd just as soon put it on him if you think it's all right," she offered hopefully.

"I'm sure it would be, but just to play safe I'd better do it. You can help me though," he said in appeasement while they walked toward the barn.

"It might be easier to use one of our sheets," Andy suggested, reluctant to see her king back in his tattered raiment.

"You've taken quite a shine to that horse, haven't you? Are you figuring to buy him?"

"Blue is beyond price," Andy said thoughtfully, entirely missing Luis's little joke, "or he would have been sold long before Pop was in such bad shape.

"Not but what I'd buy him if I could," she continued

vigorously. "After wanting and dreaming about a horse
my own for so long having Blue appear out of the blue i
well, one minute it's like manna from heaven and the ne
it's as aggravating as an itch in the middle of my back,
see him and not own him, I mean. The ranch horses ju
aren't fun any more at all."

"You've outgrown them for sure, but take it easy
you'll get quite a jolt when Pop and Blue leave," Lu
cautioned.

They talked as they worked and soon Blue was in l
nightclothes. Luis threw him some extra bedding befo
snapping out the light.

"Get a good rest while you can, Blue," Andy call
softly into the dark. "No telling when you'll hit the ro:
again."

Andy hurried to the stable as soon as Mrs. Bard releas
her children from their after-breakfast chores next mor
ing. It had been a long, lonesome night and Blue was an
ious for company, he told her in ringing accents. She r:
a little water in his bucket although wanting to do mo
for him. He needed currying, having lain down in tl
dirtiest part of his stall, but under the "hands off" polic
she was helpless.

Neither she nor Blue was satisfied. Finally Andy cou
stand it no longer. She headed for Pop's cottage where sl
found the old man sitting up in bed as pert as a chipmun

"In case you haven't heard yet," she began, "your hor:
is fine today—but lonesome."

"I'll jest bet a peck of pennies he is. Blue's more use
to hobnobbin' with me than he is with other hosses."

"What's his whole name? It isn't just Blue, is it? Maybe Blue Diamond?"

"Yo're part right. It's Blue Smoke."

"I like that. And I like him—a lot. But first I should have asked about you. How are you feeling?"

"First rate—thanks to all the fancy lookin'-after I've been gettin'. So ya like my horse, eh? He feel the same?"

"I think so. Luis says being a stranger I shouldn't go in the stall, though, with Blue, but he needs currying. You said he's gentle, didn't you?"

"Gentle as a kitten, but Luis's right. Ya *oughta* be careful with a strange horse. Tell ya what. I think I can get up this afternoon. I'll go down there with ya an' hold him while yo're groomin' him. That way the pair of ya can get acquainted while I'm around."

"Wonderful!—but are you sure you ought to get up so soon?"

"Yep, I feel fit as a kid glove now, and will 'til my old ticker begins cavortin' again. Don't worry. I'll take it easy. You'll do the work."

Andy was beside herself with joy and soon everyone on the Bar D knew that after lunch she was at last going to lay hands on Blue Smoke. She was going to curry him even. The girl whisked and frolicked and sang, but when the time came for her and Pop to go to the stable she was as well-behaved as though she were going to church, accommodating her steps to the old man's.

Hearing his owner's voice and step outside, the stallion acted nearly as delirious as Andy had been earlier, but once the old man stepped into the stall the horse seemed to realize his infirmity. Blue stood like a statue to be haltered, never moving a hoof without first seeming to make sure that he would not jostle Pop.

"All right, Andy. Ya can come in now," the latter said to the girl who had been hovering in the doorway.

With a low-voiced reassurance Andy walked up to the horse and undid the sheet. She stared at him, her heart in her eyes.

"Pretty nice hoss, eh?" Pop put her looks into words.

"Super. They just don't come any better, I guess. What's his breeding?"

"He's by Galloping Ghost and traces back to Steel Dust four times. His dam was Jennie McCue, a granddaughter of old Peter hisself."

"Jiminy! He must have the speed of a rifle shot."

"That he has. The Quarter Horse Association rates him double A, and it's no more'n he deserves."

Andy looked at Blue silently but her thoughts for once were hardly on the horse. If he had such speed, how could his owner be almost penniless? Surely, even racing against other AA horses, he should come in first often enough to win something. Inasmuch as it would be impolite to voice her thoughts she held her peace but her face was easy to read for a man whose life and livelihood had often hinged on knowing what others were thinking. His gnarled hand stroked the gleaming neck softly.

"It's not Blue's fault," Pop said as though answering her question, and Andy jumped guiltily, wondering if she had unconsciously put her thoughts into words. "He's good—too danged good. It made a man who was richer'n he was honest want to buy him. When I refused to sell at any price he spread the rumor that Blue was vicious, a killer. It was no good denyin' it, the cards were stacked against me, makin' it harder and harder for me to get a jockey. You know as well as I do the best hoss in the world can't win if he's not in the race."

"And he can't run without a rider," Andy broke in, seeing the whole set-up. "How could anyone be that low?" she added heatedly.

"Some folks who have lots of money get so set on havin' their own way, they can't stand it to want somethin' money can't buy."

"But the others must have been stupid dopes not to know Blue wasn't vicious."

"No, I was stupid and Blue was the dope," Pop corrected sadly. "Turned out I couldn't even trust my stable boy. He had his price which the would-be buyer paid for the privilege of dopin' Blue, and I was too stupid to catch on 'til Blue became almost unmanageable, even for me."

"But then wasn't it all right—if he never really hurt anybody?"

"We-ell, he did—once. By that time I was hard-up, desperate, so I took a jockey I knowed I oughtn't. He had the reputation for being crooked as a dog's hindleg. In short races, ya know, the start's about half the race. This fellow had a deal to get Blue off to a bad start an' he held a tight rein, tighter'n Blue was used to. When the other hosses broke and Blue hit that bit there was no way to go but up, an' he did. Up an' over!"

"Did it—?"

"No, it didn't kill the jockey though it'd have been no more'n he had comin' but, of course, from then on nothin' I said did any good. Blue was blackballed."

Andy's face flushed with anger at those who had wronged her two new friends. Certainly the stallion was gentle. Pop said so. "That's what the man says—" The slangy phrase for casting doubt said itself over in her brain.

"But you'd guarantee he really is OK?" she queried soberly.

"With my life. Oh, shore, he might jump or kick or rear from fright or surprise—any hoss will—but there's not a mean hair on him."

"OK, let's get on with the grooming."

Andy felt that she could read truth when she saw it. Taking the rubber currycomb in her right hand she rubbed and scrubbed vigorously along the blue coat from ears to tail on one side, then shifting to her left hand she worked her way down the other side. Scraps of bedding and manure stuck to the horse's back legs. Despite Pop's assurance, she stood well forward to curry Blue's legs.

A second going-over with the brush burnished the stallion to the polish of a gun barrel. Andy changed over to a coarse brush and soon had the short mane snapping with electricity. The tail was next and again she prudently stood to one side while she brushed the sparse, hock-length tail to similar perfection.

"There, I guess that does it. Maybe you'd better lie down again?"

"I'll set a while, but in that chair on the stoop," Pop agreed on his own terms.

Kid Broke and Lady Gentle

Pop's steps grew slower and slower on the walk to the house where he sank gratefully into a rocker. Andy perched on the porch edge and leaned against a pillar. Both were silent, one with thoughts turned to the past, the other's turned eagerly toward the future.

"What's this, a yoga meeting?" Mrs. Bard smiled at them as she came along the path. "How do you feel today, Mr. Reed? You're looking much better."

"Oh, I feel mighty pert. Not quite ready to dance a fandango though. We"—he nodded toward Andy—"have jest been down to look after my hoss."

"That's fine, but don't overdo. I was wondering if you would like to come to the dining room this evening. It's not much fun eating alone, but do as you think best."

"I will, an' thank ya again, ma'am. I'll pay ya for yore pains, of course."

"You'll do no such thing. We've just started as a dude ranch and I think as our very first guest—we never could call an old-timer like you a dude—you'll bring us luck. Everything's on the house," she finished with a flourish.

"That's mighty white of ya, ma'am, but there's one favor I'd like to ask. I don't want to vex ya but that place is too highfalutin for me, curtains and cushions an' such. Don't ya have a little room or a cubbyhole some place? Why, jest an empty stall'd suit me fine."

Mrs. Bard had unconsciously stiffened when he began, thinking that he was going to take advantage of her hospitality, but his question eased another worry. She had been wondering just what she could do if the cottage, the ranch's best accommodation, were needed.

"I might be able to work out something later, but meanwhile just don't look at the curtains and cushions." Her smile was understanding.

Andy followed her mother into the house to tell her Pop's story.

"So that's why he's in such straits when he seemed to have a good money-maker. I'd wondered whether he had gambled away his money—or spent it for drink," Mrs. Bard said with relief, only to think again. "I do hope that other man was wrong. I don't want a mean stallion around."

"Oh, Muz, Blue couldn't possibly be mean. You should see how gentle he is with Pop, and he let me curry him all over, including his back legs and tail. Why, he's gentle as a kitten—and *he* doesn't have claws."

"No claws maybe, but what he has is far more dangerous. Go and round up Jump and Val, Andy. We'll see what we can do before supper to fix a place for Pop."

"Fix what place, Muz? I wondered what you meant."

"I think we can clean out that little shack by the kitchen, put in some furniture and it'll be just fine for him."

"Jiminy, it's pretty primitive. Maybe he'll think we're trying to get rid of him."

"No, quite the opposite, I think. He'll feel more at hom
there where he's not in the way. At least it will be wall
and a roof over his head and I'm sure it's nicer—or will b
after we fix it up—than fifty per cent of the places he ha
slept the past few months. Find the children, and bring th
pick-up over so we can toss stuff on it as we sort."

Andy did as she was told and the Bard clean-up squa
fell to on the shanty. It was an old adobe building that i
the ranch's early days had been the cook's quarters onl
to be abandoned when a newer bunkhouse was built. Sinc
then, for lack of any other use, it had been a catch-all fc
anything and everything.

An imposing pile of cast-offs mushroomed in the truc
bed as they hurried back and forth with armfuls to t
added to the load.

"I certainly didn't realize what a fire hazard this plac
was. It's a good thing something has made us clear it ou
Pop's doing us a favor instead of vice versa." Mrs. Bar
drew an arm across her warm forehead, replacing moistu
with a smudge. "I guess we might leave this old chest c
drawers here. One drawer is missing but it'll give him son
place to put his things."

"If he has any," Andy agreed, thinking of his muck
mended clothes.

"That little table we can keep for a washstand sinc
there's no plumbing here. The place won't look too bad
I hope."

"It'll be fine, Muz, after we get several layers of du
off." At first Andy had not shared her mother's optimis
but now she was enchanted with the old adobe's timele

simplicity. "Soon as we get it cleared out, let's run a hose
out here and give it a good sluicing down."

"All right, but we'll have to stand the furniture outside
so it won't be soaked. Take the broom, Andy, and be
sweeping down the walls while I finish going through this
stack of old magazines. Jump, if you'll go snake the hose
around, we'll be ready by the time you get back."

The stream of water spared nothing, walls nor ceiling
nor floor. As the run-off changed from almost straight mud
to dirty water to clean water the interior improved magically.

"Sa-a-ay, this isn't half bad," Jump exclaimed. "Wish I'd
thought of it first."

"Don't worry, you may be here yet if we should get a
flock of reservations," his mother warned. "I wouldn't be
above bunking all of us in the barn if it meant that many
more paying guests."

Andy looked at their miracle with satisfaction. Both Blue
and Pop would be comfortable now. The plain adobe walls
had the quiet and solidity of the earth itself. The clean
smell of water and wet wood had replaced the former
mustiness, and a fresh breeze wandered in through the open
door and windows.

"When'll you move Pop, Muz?"

"Not until the place has thoroughly dried out. Maybe
tomorrow when you come home from school—maybe not
until Tuesday."

"Don't do it until I get home. I want to be here when
he sees it first."

Monday proved to be good wash-day weather so Pop's

cabin dried as sweet-smelling as a fresh wash. Pop wa
ready as soon as Andy, her brother and sister returned from
school. They all helped although there were few enough
possessions to be transferred to the cabin.

Flanked by Andy and her mother the old man walke
along the gravel path between the cottage and the big
house to stand at last before his new residence. Andy hel
her breath. If he liked it, he might not be in such a hurry
to leave—taking Blue with him.

"Now this's more like it," he said with satisfaction
"Nothin' flossy but downright comf'table."

It did look inviting, Andy thought. She had brought
little Navajo blanket to toss across the back of the ol
armchair that retained more comfort than style while an
other rug, well-worn but colorful, covered the board floor
ing. The cot bed was narrow but comfortable, Andy knev
from having slept on it herself at Fiesta time when they ha
a houseful. She had slipped in before this official move t
light a fire in the tiny corner fireplace so common in west
ern homes before the days of central heating.

"I'm glad you like it, Mr. Reed. Plan to stay until yo
feel perfectly able to travel. Hearts can't be hurried, yo
know."

At Pop's request Jump brought the bedroll from the car
not for the bedding but the extra clothing rolled inside

The old man was strangely silent at supper. Andy
nerves grew tighter and tighter. Surely he liked the room
he had said so several times. Was he going to tell them h
was leaving despite all their efforts to make a place for him

By dessert time she was too worried to savor Rosita's cherry pie. Pop cleared his throat apologetically and spoke just in time to save Andy's pie from her omnivorous brother.

"Yo're so good to me already, ma'am, I hate to be a botheration. I'm shore Andy won't mind—though I haven't said anythin' to her 'til I got yore go-ahead first. Blue's been havin' daily workouts so his standin' in a stall sorta worries me. Would ya mind lettin' her ride him around for me, just at a walk, so's his legs don't stiffen up or swell?"

In one swift flash glory spread across Andy's face, no

less brilliant than had she seen the Promised Land, but her mother's words snuffed out the radiance.

"I don't know about that, Mr. Reed. Stallions can be tricky and I don't want Andrea to get hurt."

"Miz Bard, ma'am, d'ya think for a minute I'd repay yore generosity by flirtin' with your daughter's safety? I'd stake my life on Blue's gentleness."

The old man's simple dignity was so sincere Mrs. Bard's doubts seemed foolish and she was ashamed of herself. She did an about-face.

"Forgive me! I'm sure you're right, but we Bards are extra nervous about accidents. Yes, she can exercise your horse for you if she's careful."

Andy barely repressed a wild, cowboy yell at her mother's decision but a quick flush of delight blossomed on her face. She would have liked to rush off to the barn that instant but she knew there would be hours of waiting for a new day, then more hours before she would be free.

Monday had been long but Tuesday was forever. She ran up the driveway after school and minutes later, face flushed and eyes dancing, presented herself at Pop's door.

"I'm ready to exercise Blue. You haven't done it yet, have you?"

"Pshaw, no! How would a stove-in old geezer like me do it? Come on."

Her heart thumped wildly with excitement as she and Pop neared the stable. Blue bugled his greeting before they entered the door and found him nodding his head up and down as if in welcome.

"Hi, fella. Guess what! You're going out for a little stroll at last," Andy chirped happily. "Say, Pop, I hope he's used to a western saddle. I don't much like the looks of that peewee racing saddle in your car."

"Oh, shore, he's used to anythin', even bareback. I've ridden him that way plenty o' times."

Luis who had been puttering in the tackroom came out with Andy's saddle and she knew he had been waiting there on purpose. While she felt his care was unnecessary, it nevertheless warmed a spot somewhere beneath her ribs. With currycomb and brush she quickly cleaned off the muscular roan to be ready for the blankets and saddle. Pop handed Luis Blue's own bridle and the horse was soon ready.

Andy hoped the men could not hear her heart thumping when it was time to mount. She stepped to Blue's left side, gathered the reins and with left foot and right hand she swung up easily. Luis had lingered carelessly near Blue's head but the horse stood motionless while Andy settled securely into the saddle, her legs snug along his side. Even motionless Andy felt the power and vitality of the horse beneath her. After the ranch horses, all of them tried and true old veterans, it was like a Cadillac compared to a Model T.

"Any particular place you want me to ride him, Pop?"

"That corral over there is empty. Ride him in there," Luis suggested before Pop could answer.

Andy recognized it for as much an order as a suggestion. She looked wistfully at the trail that bordered the creek and one that led over the hills beyond the house while she reined Blue toward the corral. Luis closed the gate behind them.

Val and Jump joined Luis and Pop, thereby making Andy's big moment bigger, for they were still committed to the ranch's remuda. Even at a walk behind corral bars she was on a plane above them. They realized it too; she could tell from Jump's first words.

"Say, Pop, would you say that Blue is 'kid broke and lady gentle'?"

Whatever he said would be wrong. If he said "yes" they too would want to ride Blue. If he said "no" it would be an admission that Andy should not be riding the stallion, but Luis who had had practice parrying Jump's questions came to the rescue.

"For some people, he is, Jump. Andy's riding him proves it, for one minute she's a kid and the next minute a lady— or almost. Don't you go getting ideas. Riding Blue is by invitation only."

"Pop, how come Blue has to have so much walking? I should think if he's a racehorse, he ought to run." Val got into the conversation with a question.

"There's an old sayin', 'Walk for muscle, gallop for wind,' an' Quarter Hosses're famous for their bulgin' muscles."

"Don't they need wind too?"

"Shore they do." Pop gave one of his rare chuckles. "Course, some folks who don't cotton up to our short hosses say they can run only 's far 's they can hold their breath. 'Tain't so though, they've got good wind."

Andy and Blue circled the corral again and again. To

some it might have been monotonous but to Andy every step of the powerful animal was a thrill. As a true Quarter Horse Blue carried his head low with little arch in his neck, for how else could he keep his eyes on a crazy cow, his head out of the way of his rider's twirling rope? The small, alert ears tipped back and forth constantly, missing no small detail of his new surroundings.

After many circuits Andy missed Luis from the group, his admission that he was satisfied about Blue's good behavior. A few minutes later her brother and sister left in search of other excitement. Pop was the only spectator, but he seemed never to tire of watching the ripple of Blue's muscles, the play of light over the shining coat.

·4·

Nomad No Longer

From that day on Andy lived in a beautiful soap-bubble world. Knowing it might burst any moment made each ride on Blue doubly precious, a few minutes of perfection snatched from a capricious fate. She no longer dreamed of buying her own horse, for after Blue Smoke anything else on four legs would be second best.

Perhaps because Andy had been vouched for by his man-god, perhaps because she just had a way with a horse, girl and stallion became fast friends at once. He welcomed her approach almost as much as he did Pop's. The threesome spent as much time together as Andy could manage, for every time she saddled Blue she wondered whether that would be her last ride before Pop decided to leave.

Although his improvement had surprised everyone, Andy insisted that he make himself comfortable on a bale of hay while she was a willing handmaiden for the stallion. The old man was not one to take advantage of an invalid's status, however, and did innumerable small chores around the house and barns, but it was Rosita, the cook, who found him most helpful. Much kitchen work is light but tedious so Pop had made a real place for himself there, preparing vegetables, washing or drying dishes and lending a hand where it was needed most.

Andy in her direct way asked him about these unsuspected talents that had everyone else wondering.

"Jiminy, Pop, how come you're so handy in the kitchen when you're an outdoor man?"

"Girl, after ya've knocked around as many years as I have, earnin' a livin' the best way ya can, ya learn a variety of things, but it actually goes back farther than that. I didn't have any sisters so my brother an' I served our time in the kitchen helpin' my mother. Now woman's work is about all I'm good for."

"Nonsense, Pop. You'll be as good as new in no time," she contradicted stoutly, only to hurry on lest he think she was trying to get rid of him. "Of course, it's best to take things slowly."

"Some things, but Blue f'r instance will be gettin' fat and lazy if we don't take care. After ya've walked him a while ya better lope him out a mite."

The rest of the world faded away the minute Andy mounted Blue, only she and Pop and the stallion being real. Just walking had been a genuine thrill until today, but now that she was going to step Blue out the preliminary walking was a nuisance and a bore.

Her big moment came. She lifted Blue into their first canter together and it was as cadenced and rhythmic as a dancer's step. Andy would not have changed places with princes or presidents.

"Send him on an' feel out his speed," Pop called from the gate.

The girl leaned forward, touching her heels to the horse that nearly jumped out from under her as he sprang forward. The surging muscles sent an electric shock through her body. She wanted to whoop and yell with exhilaration but she refrained lest it make Blue really take off.

The corral was not large enough for real speed but the pounding hoofs beat accompaniment to her heart. Dirt and pebbles driven by the thrusting hoofs spattered against the bars. After two or three circuits of their ring, Andy re-

luctantly pulled Blue back to a lope, then a walk. Her eyes sparkled and her cheeks flamed with excitement when she drew rein by Pop.

"Wow! What a horse! On a straightaway I'll bet he'd really scorch along. You've never ridden him in a race yourself, have you, Pop?"

"Not on a track. When he was younger I used to match him against some of my friends' hosses, but then my ticker began cuttin' up an' I didn't dare. I have to be content with just watchin' him run."

Blue Smoke was warmer than usual so Andy had to cool him out carefully, hovering over him lovingly until he was groomed and returned to his stall. Pop acted in the role of overseer.

"Stop by my car a minute, Andy," he said when they had finished, "and I'll show you some pictures of Blue when he was a baby."

"Great! It's hard to think of his ever being little and awkward."

" 'S funny thing, he never was really ganglin' like most colts. From the day he was foaled he's always looked like a real little hoss, every part in perfect proportion with the rest."

Pop slid into the back seat where he moved several cardboard cartons until he uncovered a little wooden chest covered with intricate carving. He unsnapped the brass latch and lifted the lid.

"What a dear little chest," Andy exclaimed. "It must be very old."

"That it is. My granddaddy on my mother's side was a

sea-goin' man aboard a clipper ship in the China trade. He brought this back to my gramma as a weddin' present. I've heard that it was filled with oriental treasures then—prob'ly they'd be priceless now, but they've all been lost—or sold. I continue the family tradition by keeping my treasures in it." Pop smiled sadly as he withdrew a packet of pictures. "This here's a picture of Blue when he was twelve hours old."

Andy and Pop's heads bent over the record of Blue's baby days, his years of growth, his maturity. Pop had just snapped the rubber band on the pictures and picked up a small sheaf of newspaper clippings when Mrs. Bard's voice aroused them.

"You're a pair! Always talking horses, thinking horses, working horses." Her smile proved she knew how they felt. "Mr. Reed, since you came I've been wondering how we got along without you and so, before you begin to think of leaving us, I'd like to make you a proposition. I haven't ready cash enough to pay you wages right now but if you would like to work for just your and your horse's keep, I'd be more than happy to have you."

Andy jammed her hands in her pockets, fists clenched. To have Blue Smoke here all the time! Pop wouldn't be able to ride him much, even if he got a lot better, so keeping the stallion exercised would be her glorious lot. Her face first paled, then flushed rosy red as she waited for Pop's answer.

"Of course, don't feel that you have to if you'd rather—" Mrs. Bard began, misreading his hesitation.

"It's not that, ma'am. I was wonderin' if I could make

myself useful enough to keep ya from gettin' stung. Already this's more like home than any place I've been for years."

"You let me worry about my bargain." Mrs. Bard smiled. "Luis agrees with me too, says you seem to be able to do everything from keeping an eye on the horses to fixing the plumbing or helping Rosita. The cabin is yours for as long as you want to stay."

"Thank ya very much. I'll—"

"Hooray, Pop! I'll help you carry your stuff in. Look, Muz, isn't this a wonderful little chest? What d'ya want me to take first?"

Andy rattled exclamations and questions like an automatic. She couldn't wait for her mother and Pop to conclude their arrangements so she hurried off to his cabin with an armload of boxes and the little chest.

A short time later Pop was a nomad no longer, for everything he owned was in one place. Even his meager possessions softened the cabin's bareness, lending a homey appearance that Andy heightened by hanging her most cherished horse picture over the fireplace.

With his new status as permanent resident Pop easily fitted in like one of the family. He took little part in their earnest discussions of ranch problems but his concern was plain to see. He rejoiced with the others when the Bar D received its first two reservations.

"I think they're honeymooners which is a good thing as they won't mind its being so quiet here," Mrs. Bard concluded. "They're to arrive next Saturday and stay through the Memorial Day weekend."

"Thank goodness! Somebody's broken the ice, maybe our luck's going to turn. I can't see why we haven't at least had a flock of inquiries. We've got a good location, our rates are reasonable—and we need dudes," Andy said soberly.

"Yes, it does seem strange that the only other nibble we've had was from a girl who brazenly asked how many unattached men guests we had. Since we've never heard from her after I answered her query, I assume her accent was on dudes rather than ranching." Mrs. Bard's tone was lightly wistful.

"Muz, there must be some gimmick we could use to make people think of the Bar D when they're thinking of duding," Andy pondered. "Just advertising isn't enough. It has to be advertising that grabs 'em and sells the Bar D."

"Such as—?"

"Oh, something like 'George Washington slept here.'"

"I know," Jump exclaimed. "We'll have bank nights and gate prizes."

"And you'll be the prize in the first package we give away, young man," his mother promised with mock severity. "Meanwhile, Andrea, until you dream up some way to dramatize the ranch, we'll be grateful for two dudes and keep hoping."

With that, dinner-table talk veered away from the ranch's problem to discussion of the Memorial Day Rodeo to be held in a neighboring town. Luis and his bay mare were entered in the calf roping but this was not enough to satisfy Andy who stoutly maintained that the ranch should be represented in every possible event.

"What else do you suggest?" her mother asked dryly. "Maybe you would like to go in for wild bull riding."

"I'll save that event for Jump," Andy parried, "but there *must* be other things."

She pulled a worn list of events from her pocket and forgot her food while poring over it. Her finger traveled down the sheet as the others heard her murmuring, "Not that, or that, or that." Shaking her head with disappointment she was about to refold the sheet when Pop reached over for it. He in turn checked it carefully while the conversation went on around him.

"It's just too bad the committee couldn't have included some events for amateurs that we could get in. Here's a perfectly wonderful place for the Bar D to get some publicity in front of hundreds of people—and nothing to enter!" Andy snorted her disgust.

"My, what a little publicity hound we have among us," Mrs. Bard smiled. "You act like a movie-struck girl who does everything she can to make herself conspicuous."

Andy was crestfallen for a moment but soon found an answer.

"Yes, I guess I am a publicity hound, but it's in an unselfish cause. I want to make the Bar D conspicuous, so people will come. I'm no more than a stage prop."

"Here's jest the ticket for ya, Andy." Pop looked up from the paper with a quizzical smile.

"What?" Andy queried cautiously.

"This 'ladies' quarter mile race.' It oughta be a cinch for ya."

"Oh, sure! I can run faster than— You don't mean—?"

"Blue Smoke, of course. Yo're used to each other. He can run an' ya can ride. What more'd a body want?"

"Just one thing—Muz's OK!"

Mrs. Bard stared at her plate as if the answer to her problem might be written in its pattern. Everyone there knew she was seeing the blue roan stallion towering in the air, crashing backwards on his jockey. Suppose Pop's love for his horse blinded him to Blue's vices? She turned toward Pop, meeting his level brown look, trustworthy as an old dog's. Her defenses wilted.

"That's certainly generous of you, Mr. Reed. Do you think Andy could handle him in a race?"

"Shore she could! She already handles him as well as I do. Oh, she'd have to practice a few quick starts. That's the biggest trick to ridin' short hosses 'cause they start right now."

"You mean I can, Muz?" For once Andy was almost speechless.

"You ought to win at a walk, Andy," Luis exclaimed enthusiastically. "There isn't a horse around here like him."

"There's a tol'able purse for the race too," Pop added.

"Good! I guess you can use the money—if I win it," Andy added modestly, having regained her powers of speech.

"Not me," Pop disclaimed. "*When* ya win it, it'll apply to Blue's keep. He might's well work for his livin' when he can."

·5·

B Plus A Equals X

Andy and Pop held a solemn conference when it was time to work Blue as to whether she should try the flat racing saddle or go on with her own western saddle. She looked at the little saddle doubtfully.

"Jeepers, Pop, I'm not sure I could stick on such a thing. It'd be terrible to just plain fall off."

"Shore enough, it would. Well, yore saddle's not as heavy as some. I guess it won't hurt to try it. You'll feel a lot better in one yo're used to."

"I can take up my stirrups so they won't be so long as I generally ride them. That'll help, won't it?"

"Yep, that'll be fine. The one thing to be careful of is the cinch. A Quarter Hoss's start calls for the stoutest girth."

Reasoning that her mother's permission to ride in the race would also permit her to ride the stallion outside the corral, Andy was all impatience to get Blue ready. She mounted and turned expectantly toward Pop only to see him walking toward the corral gate which he swung open.

"Hey, I thought we'd be doing starts today."

"Sunday's time enough. There'll still be five days 'til the

race. No use gettin' him all lathered up this far ahead. Just walkin' with a little lopin' is plenty good."

The girl was disappointed to learn that their horizons were not yet to widen but as an apprentice she could not argue with Blue's owner-trainer. Her saving sense of humor came to her aid, and she recalled her first great thrill riding Blue at a walk. Perhaps the remembered experience, but more likely the magic of being on Blue's powerful back, soon erased her discontent. She set herself to getting accustomed to the unusually short stirrups.

The different length was difficult enough at a walk but when Pop waved them on Andy, who had learned to ride when she learned to walk, understood at last how insecure a first-time rider might feel. Her stirrups threw her forward where the horn took a mean delight in poking her midriff while Blue himself felt as rough as a cork in a choppy sea. Just as she got the hang of it but before she could enjoy her hard-won comfort, Pop motioned them back to a walk.

"Blue's ready. Ya oughta show yore heels to 'most anybody. Any notion who the other entries will be?"

"Not for sure. Other years it's just been the gals from around here with the best horses they could get hold of."

"The pair of ya should win goin' away then. That'll do for today."

For Andy the time from then until Sunday when she and Blue were to work on a starting line would have dragged endlessly except that the honeymooning couple arrived promptly Saturday morning. She was delegated to be their dude wrangler. After one look at their starry-eyed preoccupation with each other, Andy saddled the two gentlest horses in the string, then stayed well ahead of them throughout the ride.

"They wouldn't have known if they'd been on mules," she reported to Luis later. "After this you can just put them on old Bess and Babe and turn 'em loose. The horses will bring them home even if the riders don't know where they are."

Early the following morning when Andy and Pop headed toward the stable, Luis and Jump also saddled horses.

"Hey, you two. The race isn't for several days. How come the cheering section?"

"You can't start a horse all alone. It's where the other horses are in the race that counts," Luis explained, "and my bay can stand a little practice. Whether it's racing or calf roping a quick start is half the win. She'll give you and Blue some real competition."

Andy was further startled to see Luis saddle another horse.

"Pop, are you going to ride too? Don't you think that's pretty reckless?"

"Don't calc'late it is. Once I feel pretty good again after a spell, jest sittin' a hoss at a walk doesn't seem to faze me. How d'ya s'pose I kept Blue in top shape?"

The four mounted and headed down creek to the big meadow where Luis said the footing was best. Andy forgot everything else in her own excitement. It flowed through the reins to Blue until he danced sideways to show he was ready. Pop dismounted at the chosen spot while the other three cantered on down field and back for a warm-up.

Blue knew something was brewing and he danced and cavorted but always under Andy's perfect control, never once attempting to bolt. Pop as official starter had drawn a line on the ground with a stick when the three returned.

"We're not shore if they'll use a startin' gate so we'll pretend we have one. Ride yore hosses up to this line an' stop 'em, flat-footed. I'll count to three an' say 'Go!' An' you scat!

"Get a good stance in yore stirrups, Andy, lean forward an' either have a fistful of mane or a strangle holt on that horn or you'll somersault right back over his tail. Ready?"

Three horses tiptoed up to the line where Pop stood with his hand raised. Andy tensed herself. One hand held the reins, the other was wound tightly into the blue-black mane. She leaned forward over Blue's neck as Pop started counting. Blue's body hardened like iron as his muscles tensed and gathered for his lunge.

"Go!"

Andy never knew whether she had time to jab her heels into Blue's side or whether he too understood the signal. He exploded as though jet-propelled and hurtled forward, a blue-steel projectile. Andy clung desperately, doggedly, though Blue's terrific charge had twisted her neck, almost made her swallow her breath.

Luis's bay mare drove forward from her haunches in a tiger-spring but quick as she was Blue's neck was in front on the second bound with his lead widening at every jump. After a short dash they drew rein and turned back toward the starting line.

"Phew! I see what you mean, Pop. It's a wonder I didn't jerk his mane out by the roots," Andy gasped.

"I don't know how you did it," Luis said admiringly,

"but I think that is without doubt the fastest get-away I ever saw. He stays fast too, once he gets under way."

"Most of it's Blue himself. Oh, shore, I've encouraged him a mite," Pop said mildly. "Ready for one more? Likely that'll be enough for ya to know each other pretty well."

The three horses circled around to walk up to the line

again. Andy braced herself. At Pop's "Go! the blue roan shot forward faster than before, proving the first start was not a fluke as well as testing the girl's horsemanship. The bay's head was at Andy's stirrup but it fell behind as she let the stallion run a ways before pulling him down.

"Hey, Luis, what'd you stop so soon for?"

"I wasn't stopping. You were just pulling away from us," the foreman said in open-mouthed amazement. "If I were a few years younger and a good many pounds lighter, Pop and I'd go campaigning with that horse. He's wearing seven-league horseshoes!"

"I'd go if Muz would let me," Andy exploded. Then like a firecracker that fizzes out she added, "But I know she wouldn't."

"Racetracks and racing are no place for a nice girl like you anyway," Luis reminded her. "Besides you're needed to help with the dudes."

"Sure, sure. I hardly have time to sleep for taking care of all the dudes we have. Hah!"

"Two more are checking in tomorrow, your mother told me just as I came out."

"There are?" Andy exclaimed with fresh cause for alarm. "Glory, I hope we don't get so busy Muz won't want me to go to the rodeo—and the race."

"Don't worry about that. The Bar D is going in a body, picnic lunch, grandstand seats and lemonade for everyone."

Pop who had remounted by the time they rode back to the starting line nodded with satisfaction.

"You and the hoss are gettin' on together fine. Now jest work him easy every day an' he'll be fit."

Between working Blue, going to school, helping around the horses and giving her mother a hand, time that Andy had expected to drag before Memorial Day whirled past miraculously fast. The evening before Memorial Day Luis returned from the city, his pick-up loaded with supplies, his head full of news.

"Guess what I heard today, Andy," he said at supper.

"If I knew what, I'd be telling you, but I give up. What?"

"As a first wedding anniversary present Mack Westby's bought Julia a fancy Quarter Horse. She figures she has that race just about in the bag."

"She does, eh? Where'd the horse come from and what's it like?"

"No sabe," Luis mimicked with an expressionless face. "They say he paid plenty of money for it but I couldn't find anyone who'd seen it—not that I didn't try hard enough."

Andy ate in silence while she thought over this new development. Resentment flared up in her that their neighbor had done such a thing, until her innate fairness came to her rescue. After all, the others might think the same thing about her riding Blue.

"So there'll be another dark horse in the race," her mother mused. "That may upset a lot of ideas."

"Muz, Luis didn't say it was a black horse," Val corrected.

"A dark horse, honey, is an expression for an unknown quantity, a horse no one knows anything about."

Andy's confidence in her horse had returned. Blue was

the equal of any Quarter Horse, in fact he was in a class by himself. Fragments of her algebra came back and she grinned happily.

"Well, it doesn't matter for I've got proof right in my algebra that Blue's going to win. The other horse is un- known quantity X and it says in the book that B plus A equals X."

"What's B plus A?" Val asked.

"Blue plus Andy, dope." Jump's air was extra lordly because he caught on.

"Just 'equals' won't do, Andy," Luis teased. "We don't want any dead heats. You've got to be better or it'll be a tie."

"It won't be a tie," Andy vowed grimly. "Blue's got to make a name for his new home, the Bar D."

That thought fortified her during the coming hours: a restless evening but a sound sleep, early morning prepara- tions and finally the trip to the fairgrounds. The dudes wanted to ride in the morning parade through town that advertised the rodeo, so Luis put the stock rack on the flat- bed truck in order to haul their horses and his bay. Blue Smoke, however, went in his own trailer, hitched to the pick-up truck driven by Mrs. Bard.

The Bar D contingent arrived in good time. As soon as parade preparations were complete Andy and Luis went looking for Julia Westby's new Quarter Horse. They prowled up one line of stalls and down another without any success until Luis met a crony who directed them to the remotest section of stalls.

"Here, these must be the Westby stalls all right, Luis. That's their truck and trailer," Andy pointed out.

Peering over one stall door after another they found a white-stockinged sorrel gelding that was Quarter Horse through and through. They stared in silence, each one trying to find a flaw in the sorrel but failing. He looked every bit as good as Blue.

"Well, races aren't won on looks anyway," Andy said philosophically. "It's what a horse has inside that counts. If I don't butch it up somehow, I know Blue will get there first."

Andy wished she had never thought of the possibility of her ruining the race, for it cast a shadow across the whole day. Although she got a momentary thrill seeing the Bar D riders in the parade, all the other fancy turnouts moved past in a haze. A stomach full of butterflies left no room for the delicious lunch Rosita had worked so hard and long to prepare. Even the rodeo's opening events were just so many shadows.

Mrs. Bard was feeling a strain too but she was able to smile, if somewhat tightly, and wish Andy good luck when she and Pop left to saddle Blue. As soon as Andy went to work on the horse her nervousness eased up, leaving her completely once she settled into the saddle. Confidence in herself and her horse returned.

"Walk him jest long enough to loosen him up," Pop directed, "then lope him around the track easy, lettin' him out a little at the finish. Then jest keep him movin' 'til race time. Oh, yes, another thing, take him clockwise of the track for warm-up. When you turn him the other way he knows he's going to run."

"Any special way I should ride him in the race?"

"Jest get out in front an' stay there. Blue'll do the rest."

Races and rodeo events were alternated, leaving the track clear in plenty of time for the next runners to warm up. Andy set about carrying out Pop's orders but she was not too preoccupied to savor the admiring glances cast at the stallion as she took him out on the track.

Blue cantered easily, so easily Andy wondered fleetingly whether he would run when the time came, then dismissed the thought as disloyal. She saw four other girls, all of them older than herself, warming up their horses without seeing the Westby entry.

"Guess the dark horse is the one to beat, Blue. These others don't look as if they'd push you much. OK, let's slow down. You're just right for a run."

As if waiting for her to be ready the loudspeaker called all entries in the ladies' race to report to the starting gate on the back stretch. A gate was nothing new to Blue. He walked up to it, entering the number three stall like the veteran he was. Andy whispered a word of thanks to him, for she would not have relished the experience of fighting her horse in such close quarters.

Julia Westby had drawn number one post position. Her horse too accepted the gate calmly but not so the other four entries. The ones on either side of Andy snorted and pulled back, number two bolted on through but his rider backed him in again. The fourth horse finally entered under pressure, five likewise, but number six said she would have none of it. After much tussling the officials decreed that six must start on the far end outside the gate.

Horses and riders crouched tensely. At the one instant when all horses were faced forward, their feet on the ground, the starter sent them off. Blue surged out with a tremendous leap that should have put him in the clear but the second horse kangaroo-leaped and came down sideways, jostling the roan stallion at the same instant number four swerved too quickly toward the rail. Either blow alone might have knocked Blue off his feet but the simultaneous shocks pinned him between them as if in a vise while Julia Westby on her fleet sorrel shot into the lead.

The offenders ricocheted to either side. Blue caught his stride, picking up speed so fast it was hard for Andy to maintain her forward position. The roan thundered after the leader, his thrusting back legs driving him onward with express train speed. Andy could see that the sorrel was no longer gaining ground. She yelled to Blue in Pop's words.

"Get out in front! Get out in front!"

The stallion answered her with a new burst of speed that ate up one length but the sorrel was fast too, holding his advantage momentarily until Blue's great strength began to assert itself. The gap narrowed gradually to two lengths. Rounding the turn into the home stretch Andy went wild that victory might not be hers.

"Hi-yaaah, Blue! Come on. Come on. You can do it!"

She felt him respond as his drumming hoofbeats rapped out an even faster tempo that ate into the narrowing margin. Julia heard them on her heels and went to the whip but her sorrel had nothing left to give. He tried, but the

powerful stallion seemed to be running him down. T
finish line raced toward them even faster. Andy was ri
ing with all she had, body, voice, reins, as jump by jur
Blue Smoke overhauled the sorrel to reach his flanks, I
shoulder.

Head and head the two horses flashed in front of t
grandstand, each one giving his utmost for his rider. Blu

great heart decided it. He pushed his flaring nostrils across the line in front of the fast-tiring sorrel.

Throughout the race the stands had been in a riot that swelled to a higher pitch when Blue began his stretch run, but it became a deep-throated roar when he flashed home the winner. The stallion's rush carried them down the track far past the Westby entry before Andy could ease him down. She was not sure herself whether Blue had won but, turning, she loped back in time to hear the announcement.

"Ladies and gentlemen, you have just seen a ree-al horse race. The winner is number three, Blue Smoke, ridden by Andy Bard of the Bar D Ranch—"

She fell forward on his mane to encircle the sweaty neck in a bear hug.

"You did it, Blue. You did it in spite of everything. But close finishes like that aren't good for your boss's heart, big boy. Better watch it after this."

·6·

Killer?

The crowd roared its welcome to Andy and Blue wh
they rode up in front of the grandstands. She did her b
to contain her happiness but it radiated from every po
sang itself through a restrained "Thank you" to a comp
mentary official, flashed from her eyes like a beacon wh
the Bar D cheering section rose to salute her. The form
ities complete, Andy turned Blue toward the stables wh
she and Pop cared for the sweating hero like a baby.

"Did I ride him all right, Pop?"

"Must've. Ya won. I didn't dare watch it but I could
from the whoopin' and hollerin' it was a close one."

They were still occupied with the horse when the c
roping event came up so they missed Luis's winning p
formance but they heard afterward how his bay flash
from the barrier to overhaul the calf ten jumps later. Lu
loop went true. He leaped from his horse, threw the c
to the ground where with lightning twists he wrapped a
tied the calf's feet together in record time. Again the sp
tators heard the Bar D's name coupled with a winner.

Andy's greatest reward, since the money winnings w
to Pop who in turn gave them to Mrs. Bard for the hors
keep, was the unspoken admission that Blue Smoke was

vicious. Thenceforth she felt that she would have to answer
only to Pop on where and when she rode Blue.

The day after the race Andy did not see Pop until after
lunch since Blue was to have a holiday. She was lounging
on the porch while waiting for the dudes to decide whether

they wanted to go for a ride when the old man came
around the house. In his arms he carried the little carved
chest.

"Here, Andy, this's yores," he said without preamble,
"for provin' that Blue's not mean or hard to handle. That
was a big favor ya did us."

"You did me the favor, Pop. I don't need anything. That
race was the biggest thrill I ever had. Thanks for even
thinking of the chest, but you keep it."

"No, it's yores. What does an old man need with somethin' like this? If I'd ever had a little girl, it'd have been

hers. Now there's no one I want to have it more than you.

He set it in her lap. For a moment she could not speak
the loneliness in his voice was so unashamed. Her hand
caressed the wood softly.

"But what about the treasures you kept in it?"

"They don't mind what kind of box they're in. A shoe
box is jest as good. It's yores," he repeated stubbornly.

"Thank you ever so much, Pop. I can't begin to tell you
how much it means to me. I'll keep it always—and I'll keep
my treasures in it too."

They sat in silence, Andy toying with the brass hasp of
the Chinese chest, her thoughts whirling like clouds across
the sun, one moment bright, the next moment gray, while
she wondered what was behind Pop's gesture. Then he
spoke.

"S' long's I've made up my mind I might as well tell you
the rest. If anythin' should happen to me, I intend that
you'll have Blue too."

This time Andy was speechless. That Blue, her dream
horse, might ever be really hers when— She came up solidly
against the implication of ownership.

"But—"

"Don't fret, girl. The both of us know that any breath
might be my last. I'm not worryin'—I've lived a long life
already—but until now not bein' shore what'd happen to
Blue has been the worst. Lots o' people are so afraid of
stallions they beat 'em first to show who's boss but I know
how you are with him. Ya like each other, prob'ly in time
he'll think as much of ya as he does me."

"That's the greatest compliment I've ever had in my life

Pop. Owning Blue would be more than I ever dreamed of, but I'm sure you and he will be pals for a long time. Why, just since you've been here you seem a hundred per cent better."

"Yes, I reckon I'm some better, but I figgered now was the time to tell you. His papers—"

They looked up as the screen door opened and the dudes stepped out, dressed for a ride.

"Are the horses ready, Andy?"

"Glory, no! I wasn't sure you wanted to ride, but it won't take a minute. Come on down to the corrals. We'll be ready in jig time.

"Take it easy until I come back, Pop. We can talk about Blue then, but thanks heaps for the treasure chest."

Impulsively she stooped and dropped a quick kiss on the leathery face.

"Blue's yores when he's no longer mine. Nothin' more to talk about," the old man called after them, one hand softly cupping his cheek.

Andy was all business as she saddled up horses for the four dudes and herself. Getting the right saddle and bridle on the right horse for the right person filled her mind completely, but once they mounted and started down the trail she picked up her interrupted train of thought. One moment she wanted to sing and shout that Blue might one day be hers—only to have the full meaning douse her exuberance.

There was no catch, however, to her ownership of the little chest. She reveled in remembering its intricate carving, its pleasing proportions, its strange fragrance and aura

of far places. She busied her mind with planning which o
her most cherished possessions would qualify for the ches

All four dudes, the Bar D's entire guest list, were reluc
tant to turn the horses toward home. One trail led to ar
other and it was nearly suppertime before the cavalcad
turned back. Andy's lightning glance showed Blue's sta
empty so she turned to survey the corrals, thinking h
might have been turned out to loosen up his muscles. Sti
no horse. She called to Luis who was over by the calf per

"Hey, where's Blue?"

"Pop took him out for a little ride. Said he felt so muc
better he wanted to feel his horse under him again. H
rode off into the upper pasture somewhere."

Andy could appreciate the impulse that made Pop war
to sit his own horse once more but she was none the le
anxious. Despite her cheery reassurances she knew that h
was a sick man.

"How long ago did he leave?" she queried when Lu
came to help unsaddle.

"Oh, not very long. Don't worry," Luis counsele
drawing his watch from his pocket. "Sa-ay, time's gon
faster than I thought. It has been quite a while. I hope—

It was Andy's turn to reassure. "He's probably just sit
ting under a tree some place, smoking and thinking. Any
way, if anything had happened, we would know becaus
Blue'd come home."

They puttered and fidgeted around the stables waitin
for the absent pair to show up. Andy began cleaning tac
to keep herself busy, but her ears strained for the sound o
hoofbeats. Footsteps crunched outside on the gravel an

Andy, jumping to the door, almost knocked her mother down.

"Where's Pop, Andy? Rosita is fit to be tied because he hasn't shown up to help with supper."

"He went out for a ride on Blue while I was gone, Muz. Luis said he rode into the upper pasture but it seems as if he ought to be back by now. Do you think anything's wrong? Should I ride out to see? He seemed fine this afternoon when he gave me the chest and told me Blue was to be mine—"

"When he what?" Mrs. Bard gasped.

Andy recounted the conversation she'd had with Pop earlier in the day.

"I suppose the thought of leaving Blue sometime made him want to ride him a little—but it does seem as if he ought to be home by now."

Mrs. Bard tried to seem unconcerned but she too joined the vigil by the barn.

"Do you think we ought to go looking for him, Muz? He'd feel awfully foolish about it."

"Well, he hasn't actually been gone so long but I do think it's strange he wasn't back in time to help Rosita. That's not like him, he has been so very anxious to do his part. Yes," Mrs. Bard took command. "I think you should, Andy —no, you had better go and help Rosita get supper. Luis, you ride out and see what you can see."

In her eagerness to scan the upper pasture Andy practically walked backwards to the house where she reported Pop's nonappearance to Rosita and the hungry dudes who by then were cleaned up for supper. This hint of drama

was enough to send them back to the corrals. Meanwhi
Luis saddled a horse and rode out to search for the truan

Mrs. Bard lingered at the barn. Luis had ridden but
short way into the pasture when his horse threw up i
head and snorted. Blue burst over the hill, galloping madl
the empty saddle jouncing, the broken bridle reins slappin
his neck and chest.

Although Luis wheeled and followed as fast as he coul
Blue flashed through the gate into the lane well ahead. Mr
Bard ran toward the thundering hoofbeats only to pre
back against the fence before the fear-maddened stallion
charge. He was but a few yards away when a terrifie
scream behind her dispelled all thoughts of her own safety
One of the women guests had also started down the lan
Turning to flee from the stallion's rush her ankle twiste
and she sprawled directly in his path.

Quicker than thought, for under less stress Mrs. Bar
would have known better, she yanked off her apron an
sprang forward. Blue was almost abreast of her as she bran
dished the white cloth at him with one hand while sh
snatched for the dangling reins with the other.

Instinct ruled Blue completely, at first the unreasonin
urge to run when frightened, then his instinctive reactio
to sudden danger. Striking at this unexpected attack, h
foreleg flashed out lethally and ripped the apron from Mr
Bard's grasp to carry it down under his plunging hoof
Her face whiter than her apron had been, Mrs. Bard fe
back against the fence as the horse cut to one side of th
woman cowering in his path.

Afterward no one remembered any noise but there ha

been sufficient commotion to bring Andy running from the kitchen. Part of the drama she missed but at the moment only one fact mattered. Blue was loose.

"Whoa, Blue. Whoa!" she called, hurrying toward him.

"Get away from him, Andy," her mother cried. "He's vicious. He'll kill you."

Andy halted, dumbfounded. What had come over her mother? Blue? Vicious?

"But, Muz—"

"Andrea! Do as I tell you. Luis can catch him—or shoot him for all I care."

Andy stepped back, impressed in spite of herself by the near-hysteria in her mother's voice, while Luis attempted to catch the stallion. But horses are by nature nervous creatures which, once thoroughly frightened, become more and more terrified by their own fears.

Blue was no exception as he faced a hostile world. Once Luis might have trapped him when he raced into the sheltering barn but the stall door was closed and he lunged into the open again, nearly running the man down.

"I'll catch him, Muz. Please let me."

"Stay where you are," her mother commanded curtly.

Little by little Blue's panic was allayed by familiar surroundings. His rushes were not so frantic, his halts more frequent when he stood trembling violently, the sweat coursing in rivulets down his legs, from his belly.

Still Luis was unable to capture the horse. Each time he would have walked up to him Blue wheeled to threaten the man with his back legs and muscular quarters. This could have gone on indefinitely, for once a loose horse

adopts such tactics only a novice or a fool would wal
into range.

"Muz, you've got to let me help. You know I can d
more with Blue than anyone except Pop—and he needs ou
help out there."

Mrs. Bard's fears for her guests' and family's safety afte
her own narrow escape had blotted all other thoughts from
her mind until Andy's words recalled her to reason. And
sensed her mother's indecision.

"Please, please, Muz."

Luis too seemed to share Andy's confidence in her ability
for he looked toward Mrs. Bard for an answer. At last sh
nodded jerkily. Andy strolled toward the horse, her han
outstretched.

"Whoa, Blue. Steady, Blue. Here, Blue. Come on, Blue.

The girl's voice and the repetition of his name was o
on rough waters. He turned to face her steady approacl
Imperceptibly his fluttering nostrils stilled and the white i
his eye vanished until he looked like the Blue she ha
known. At last after breathless seconds she was able to gras
the broken reins.

The instant Andy caught the horse Mrs. Bard marshale
her forces.

"Give him to Luis, Andrea. Luis, I'll have the pick-u
here by the time you've stabled the beast and we'll go fo
Pop." Mrs. Bard ran toward the shed that housed the pick
up but turned for one last shot that pierced her daughte
to the heart. "And you, Andy, don't you dare touch tha
horse."

"Oh, Muz—"

"There's no time to argue. Just leave him alone."

Luis clapped Blue in his stall where he pulled off saddle and bridle and hastily tossed a sheet over the dripping horse before Mrs. Bard skidded the truck to a halt at the barn door.

"Grab those horse blankets, Luis. We may not need them but we'd better be ready."

From the doorway Andy watched the truck drive down the lane and swing into the pasture, jouncing roughly across the uneven ground. The rush of events left her breathless yet she sensed that the worst was still to come, for she knew Blue well enough to realize that no ordinary mishap could have so demoralized him. It was not long before she saw the pick-up crawling back through the field, her mother sitting in the truck bed beside Pop's inert form.

"Is he—is he—?" she faltered, unable to say the next word, as the makeshift ambulance passed the barn.

"Yes, I'm afraid so." Mrs. Bard's somber expression told more than her words.

When all was quiet Andy left the barn to run for her own room's sanctuary. There on the front porch where she had left it—how many ages ago?—was the little Chinese chest. She hugged it to her in a tight embrace as though there was solace in its sharp corners and unyielding sides.

Gaining her room, she fell across the bed. Though she had known Pop no more than a few weeks she had been closer to him than most people. Their love for Blue had drawn them together quickly.

In the back of her mind she knew that she cried not so much over Pop's passing but for his years of struggle and disappointment and heartbreak. Surely death would be kinder to him than life since his greatest worry, that of Blue's future, had just been settled.

·7·

Ward of the Court

Slowly Andy grew calmer. The house was quiet—quiet as death, flashed through her mind. From her window she could see the late sunlight lingering on the mountain tops. To her astonishment she realized that she was hungry, that they had never had supper.

"How can I be hungry but not want to eat?" she wondered as she moved toward the dining room. By the tables she could tell that the dudes, Val, and Jump had eaten but no one else. A fresh lump came in her throat at the sight of Pop's place still laid at the table. She whirled and started for the door again just as Mrs. Bard entered.

"There you are, Andy. I wondered what had become of you."

"What've you been doing, Muz?"

"Oh, lots of things," her mother answered vaguely. "I wonder what Rosita has managed to keep hot for us. Let's eat in the kitchen. It'll save a lot of work."

Rosita's smiles and stock of chatter were conspicuously absent that evening and, seeing her red-rimmed eyes, Andy thought that Pop had been paid his highest tribute. It was bright and warm there in the kitchen and Andy ate more

than she had ever expected to. Mrs. Bard hurried throug
her meal.

"Andy dear, will you find the children and see to gettin
them into bed and asleep? There'll be cars driving in an
out but don't let it upset you. I'll talk to you about
tomorrow."

"Whose cars, Muz?"

"Principally the doctor's—he has to come back for th
coroner's inquest—the coroner's, and the undertaker's.

"Inquest! Don't they know what happened?"

"Yes, dear. It's just routine. Now go and see if you ca
round up the others."

Andy found them in the living room with their guest
though it was anything but a cheerful gathering. Eve
Jump's bubbling exuberance had been crushed by the trag
edy so he raised no protest at being herded off to bec
Both he and Val were too keyed up for sleep, howevei
Andy remembered the soothing effect poetry had alway
had on her.

"I'll tell you what. Val, you can sleep in the other be
in Jump's room and I'll read you some poems until you ge
sleepy."

"We-ell, what're you going to read?" her brother aske
warily.

"That's for me to decide. Get ready for bed—don't for
get to brush your teeth—and Val and I'll come in."

While her sister was undressing, Andy hurried to he
own room for her English books before they returned t
Jump's room. There, bright-eyed as white mice Val an
Jump lay back on their pillows. Andy wondered whateve

had made her think she could read them to sleep with poetry, yet she had to try something. She chose the selections carefully, beginning with Kipling. At first Jump refused to be wooed by "sissy stuff" but after the first poem he realized that each poem was a story in itself and was won. Andy dipped into Longfellow, Whittier, Frost, Benét, Noyes until her lilting voice reading the musical lines lulled the two to sleep as surely as music.

Back in her own room Andy wished that someone would read her to sleep. She got ready for bed but the day's happenings kept parading before her eyes. Time after time her mind flashed back to her last real picture of Pop standing on the porch, his hand tenderly cupping his wrinkled cheek where she had dropped so quick and casual a kiss.

For the first time, event had piled on event so rapidly, she realized she had never opened the Chinese chest. She sat cross-legged on the bed, solemnly unfastened the catch and lifted the lid. Pop had removed his belongings with the exception of one slip of paper, but it was nothing more than a list of horses' names two of which were underlined. She wondered briefly whether Pop had bet on them, and if he had, had he won any money? She hoped so, for she was sure he could have used it.

Andy somehow felt that the chest would be lonely if it were left empty overnight so before getting into bed she put in some pictures and keepsakes of her father's, an all-A report card she had once had, souvenirs of trips the family had taken, some mementoes of school fun. Then she was able to sleep.

The next two days whirled past in a confusion of strange

faces and stranger events. Only her mother's stern admonition that first morning stood out afterwards with spotlight clearness.

"Andy, I want your promise not to touch that horse."

"Muz, you're upset—"

"Not another word, Andrea. The stallion is vicious, a potential killer, and unless you give me your word I may be forced to have Luis shoot him."

"He's not vicious. Why, you saw how he let me walk right up to him. What makes you think he's so mean?"

"Two things. First, he dragged Pop—we found his shoe with the laces burst out several yards from Pop. Then when I tried to catch the brute he struck at me."

"He struck at you!" This damaging evidence Andy had not heard before. She was aghast.

"Yes, another inch or two and he'd have caught me."

"Oh, Muz! S'posing he'd hurt you?" Andy was more frightened than had the danger been her own. To forget the chill her mother's words produced she hurried to another topic. "But Blue's mine now and nobody—"

"That's another thing, Andy," her mother interrupted gently. "I don't know whether he really is yours. Unless Pop put it in writing you'll have nothing but a verbal gift, and legally it may not hold up. Promise?"

"I promise—until we can talk it over more."

Andy's pledge, though dragged out reluctantly, satisfied Mrs. Bard who hurried away to other responsibilities, but her mother's words stirred a new worry in Andy's mind.

Pop's last wish was that Blue have a good home, Andy's home, and neither the law nor her family must interfere. She scowled with the intensity of her thoughts. Surely Pop had taken precautions to see that the horse was hers. But had he?

"From the look on your face, those thoughts must be worth two bits."

Luis's voice made Andy, her nerves trigger-tight, jump. She recovered quickly to unburden her troubled spirit with a rush of words.

"Luis! Muz says Blue's vicious, that he struck at her."

"Yes, I saw him. I was right behind."

Until then Andy had hoped desperately her mother was mistaken, that she might have interpreted some other action as a strike, but Luis was not to be fooled.

"I can hardly believe it. Oh, Blue, Blue, how could you?" Andy wailed.

"Well, it was this way." The foreman's brisk tones reconstructed the scene for Andy who listened with mounting hope through his final, "—the setting sun was shining full in Blue's face so when she jumped out of the shadow at him, waving her apron, I reckon he was pretty much spooked."

"Sure he was, scared to death and he struck out blindly to protect himself," the girl mused. "Any horse would have done the same. He didn't know what it was. It's not as if he did it in what the newspapers call 'cold-blood.' Muz didn't tell me that."

"It all happened so fast she probably doesn't realize it herself."

Andy was silent a moment, savoring her relief until the other prong of her dilemma jabbed her.

"Another thing, Luis, Muz says maybe Blue won't be mine after all—I don't have anything in writing. If only those dudes hadn't come out just as he was telling me. He'd just said, 'His papers—' but never got any further. All I have is his word."

"Well," the foreman began cautiously, wanting Andy to have the horse of her heart yet realizing that his employer was afraid of Blue and did not want her daughter to own him, "if you have witnesses they might—but they may have gone by now. They were leaving right after breakfast."

"Their statements! Sure! Sure!" Andy cried in full flight.

She ran for the living room. No dudes nor luggage. The porch too was empty. Their cars—a quick glance disclosed them just pulling away.

"Hey, wait a minute. Hey, wait, I want to talk to you."

Andy plunged down the steps to babble her story to the guests who were no longer surprised by anything at the Bar D. Her beseeching look could not be denied. The quartet returned to the living room where they wrote, signed and witnessed for each other.

Pop's short funeral retained the simple dignity of the old man himself. In her mind Andy had already said her good-byes to her friend, and now her determination had hardened. Pop had wanted her to have his horse, so no one was going to take Blue away.

Andy's confidence was considerably shaken when the coroner returned to take charge of Pop's personal belongings. His car and trailer were to be sold to cover his last expenses and other than the battered tack there was nothing of value but Blue Smoke. The coroner, a city man, was clearly averse to impounding an ill-tempered stallion which, temporarily at least, made him receptive to Andy's claim.

"Have you anything from the deceased in writing to prove your contention that he gave the horse to you?"

"Not yet. He had just said, 'His papers—' when we were interrupted, so I feel that somewhere in his belongings are the horse's registration papers and something signing them over to me."

"It won't take long to find out. Perhaps at the same time we'll find some clue to any heirs he may have had."

"He never had a daughter anyway," Andy said positively. "He told me so."

Mrs. Bard, Andy and Mr. Hedges, the coroner, went to Pop's cabin to search his possessions. Habit is so strong that Andy almost knocked before entering, but the man walked right in. Pop's presence was everywhere, in the orderly arrangement on the washstand, his pipe and tobacco beside the ash tray, his spectacles lying across a still-open magazine.

One bureau drawer held everything that had been in the chest. Pictures, some old and faded, some fairly recent, were carefully tied together. The newspaper clippings of Blue's career were in a packet; a cigar box held an assortment that only Pop would value, sales slips, memos to himself, a lock of dark hair. This made Mr. Hedges pause.

"There has been someone he cared about enough to save some hair," he said with weighty significance.

"I think that's mane or foretop hair," Andy said, barely repressing a nervous laugh. "Not Blue's though, maybe his mother's."

"Strange that the deceased had no wallet. Every man carries a billfold of some sort."

Andy's mouth opened to say Pop had had one at the rodeo the day before his death but she clamped her jaws together quickly. If she said that, they might be suspected of stealing it. Her silence was tacit agreement with her mother's conjecture.

"Mr. Reed had little enough money. Perhaps he felt one unnecessary."

There was one clue, the rough draft of a letter Pop had evidently written, that shone out through the meaningless keepsakes with a patient sadness.

Dear Son:

I have continued to think of you that way although you left home so young and have spent the time between trying to forget you ever had a father or mother. (Thank God she died before you had managed to break *every* rule we tried to teach you!) However, as you say, it's probably for the best to go our separate ways and forget that by an accident of fate we are related. You need never worry that I'll ask for help again and, to make it easier for you, I will do all I can to lose myself—even this postmark is false as I am asking a friend to mail my letter many miles from here.

Your erstwhile
Father

P.S. I should never have bothered you anyway. My health is fine again. Seems there was nothing wrong with my heart after all—just a little indigestion.

"Poor, poor Pop," Andy quavered.

"What a reward for a long, hard life," her mother sighed.

"That proves he had a son," the coroner said sagely. "Now to find him."

"Find him!" the two Bards exclaimed. "After he refused to help Pop when he was sick and quite plainly seems to have said he didn't want anything more to do with him?"

"The law is not interested in family quarrels. His son, without evidence to the contrary, is his legal heir."

"But his only other property is the horse," Andy pointed out, "and Pop left him to me."

"Andy, dear, I know how much it means to you now, overwrought as you are, but stop and think. What would

we do with a vicious stallion here? Let's just let Mr. Hedge
take him away with the rest of Pop's effects."

"Oh, Muz, he isn't vicious. And he's *mine*. The last word
Pop ever said to me were, 'Blue's yores when he's no longe
mine. Nothin' more to talk about.' "

"Have you anything at all to support your claim, Mis
Bard?"

Andy was too excited to see it just then but her mothe
thought the coroner seemed eager to have an excuse, any
excuse, for not being responsible for the stallion.

"Yes, I have. These."

To Mrs. Bard's surprise Andy pulled from her pocke
the four dudes' statements and thrust them at Mr. Hedges
He read them over carefully, tapped the papers thoughtfully on his knee, reread them while pondering deeply
Mrs. Bard waited hopefully for his verdict. After all, the
loss of the stallion would be a shock to her daughter bu
one that time would heal, while stabling a savage horse
would be a constant threat to themselves and their guests

"That's a good try, Andy," her mother said lightly, "but
I'm afraid Mr. Hedges won't think it's satisfactory proof.'

"Quite the contrary, Mrs. Bard. In some cases it migh
not be considered conclusive evidence but this case does
not follow the usual pattern. First, though there is pre-
sumed to be an heir we have not the remotest idea where
or who he is; second, this young lady not only raises the
question of ownership but is able to produce unbiased proof
as to the validity of her claim; third, there are no funds ir
the estate to care for the horse, yet he is too valuable ar

animal for a forced sale which might not realize a fraction of his worth."

"You mean—" Andy was too breathless to go on.

"Yes, I think the best solution is to recognize your rights in the matter while at the same time protecting a possible heir. The horse will remain here as, you might say, a 'ward of the court,' by which I mean you cannot sell or otherwise dispose of the animal. Except for that restriction he is yours to use."

Thinking it over later, Andy chuckled at realizing how hard her mother and Mr. Hedges had each tried to get rid of the stallion. At the moment she was too excited for any such analysis.

"Oh, thank you, Mr. Hedges. Thank you so much. I don't think he'll have to be a ward of the court for long. I'm sure I'll find his papers pretty quick together with whatever Pop left to prove Blue belongs to me. Muz, isn't it wonderful. To think that Blue is really mine—well, almost mine. Wait'll I tell Jump."

Andy shot out of the door looking for someone to share her good news with. Hours later, in answer to the supper bell, she came strolling back from the stables with such a happy look on her face her mother suspected insubordination.

"Andrea Bard, what have you been doing?"

"Talking to Blue. Why?"

"You gave me your solemn promise not to touch that beast, yet now you've gotten us saddled with him for heaven knows how long, you deliberately disobey me. For that—"

"Jeeps, Muz, don't get your dander up so fast. I've jus
been sitting on a box talking to him. You never said
couldn't even *speak* to him, did you?"

"Well, no, but I want you to leave him alone. He's jus
plain bad."

"Now wait a minute, Muz. You're blaming Blue fo
something that's not his fault. He may have dragged Po
as you say, but how can you be sure Pop wasn't already
dead? If he had a heart attack and fell—and I'm sure he di
or he'd have kicked clear of the stirrup—it's enough to mak
any horse bolt. Old Sam himself would do it this minute.

Andy paused for breath, only to plunge on.

"As for striking at you, I realize it looks bad but i
you'll just stop to look at it his way you'll understand
Blue was already scared silly and didn't see you there by
the fence, so when you jumped out of the shadow at him
he didn't know it wasn't a mountain lion or a bear or—or
something. His first involuntary reaction was to defend
himself—like the old-time westerners who'd shoot first and
talk later."

"Phew! Andy, you'd better be a lawyer if you've got
many more speeches like that one in you." Jump's raillery
released the tension in a laugh.

"It's no use making excuses for the horse, Andrea," her
mother said as soon as the laughter died. "He's dangerous,
downright dangerous. If he struck once in surprise he'd do
it again, only he mightn't miss."

"Luis agrees with me, don't you, Luis?" Andy appealed
to the silent foreman who was quietly minding his own
business.

"I don't care what Luis or any of you think. Blue struck at me. He's just no good and you are not to touch the horse until we know beyond any doubt that he is safe."

"But how're we ever going to know, Muz? Blue can't tell—you wouldn't believe him if he did—but I'd guarantee even a baby'd be safe right there in his stall."

"Maybe yes, maybe no. But my baby's going to be safe—outside his stall." Mrs. Bard slipped her arm through Andy's who knew when she was licked. "Now how about some food? Rosita has been biting her fingernails ever since she rang the bell."

·8·

Skeleton in the Closet

So began a very trying period for everyone at the Bar [
but for Andy most of all. Night and day she could think [
nothing else but where Pop could have put Blue's regi
tration papers. Had they been in any ordinary place th
coroner would have found them, anyone could have, [
he had put them somewhere else, intending to tell her b
no one else. That meant it would have to be a place th
was safe yet accessible to her at any time.

The day after the coroner's visit Andy stood in th
middle of Pop's cabin, her eyes closed, trying to make he
self feel and think like Pop. Where? In such a bare litt
place there was scant room for secrecy. The floor? Sh
bent over like a caricatured detective to scan each boai
minutely but it was easy to see that the nails and old boar
had not been disturbed since the day they were laid.

The bed? Not likely, since the frame was iron and sh
doubted that Pop would mutilate another's property
serve his own purpose. Nevertheless she pulled the cove
back but not so much as a darned spot showed in th
ticking.

The wall—a loose brick! Andy flew at the walls, feelin
testing, probing, looking for all the world as if she we

about to climb one. Once her heart flipflopped with hope only to return to its steady thudding when she found the brick could not be dislodged by any means.

Back at the door where she had started Andy paused, thoughtfully sucking a finger she had skinned in her enthusiasm. Where, oh, where, could Pop have hidden the papers? She sat in Pop's old armchair and rocked, concentrating on feeling like someone else, but it was no use.

"Maybe I'll dream it," she thought aloud. "Lots of things are solved by dreams."

She deliberately ate a strange meal that evening, its highlight being plenty of pickles and ice cream. Mrs. Bard who had many other things on her mind finally became aware of her daughter's odd diet.

"Goodness, Andy, have you been around goats lately? Your eating habits have become just as unusual."

"No, I'm eating this stuff so's I'll dream where Pop put Blue's papers. It must be some place easy and I'm hoping my unconscious will tell me."

"If it does, you'll be too unconscious yourself to know it. Take it easy."

As Andy's "unconscious" remained aloof, the next day she ransacked the barn from top to bottom and one end to the other. Still no luck.

"Here, you'll need a pair of hay hooks if you decide to move that fifty ton of hay there," Luis said soberly but with a gleam in his eye.

"Oh, Luis, where could Pop have hidden them?"

"Have you thought about his car and trailer?"

"No, Luis, no! They couldn't be in either of them they've been sold."

"They've been sold all right, but that's no guarantee th papers didn't go with them."

Pure panic snatched at Andy's heart and squeezed tight. If he had— If they did— Logic asserted itself as And went back over her reasoning. No, car and trailer were to transient for Pop to have done that. He surely would hav picked somewhere that she had access to.

How easy it would have been to wave the papers an bill of sale under Mr. Hedge's nose, saying with authority "He's mine. See!"

Andy went to her room and carefully took everythin out of the chest again for the fifth time, but only the dog eared slip of paper had come with it. She strained her ear as she rapped the chest all over, its sides, its lid, its bottom but she heard only the hard, unyielding sound of knuckle on wood, nothing to disclose a hidden compartment.

Final examinations and last-day-of-school exercises passe almost unnoticed by Andy (except for her report card) On top of her mounting uneasiness at not finding the paper as quickly as she had expected, Andy grew more and mor indignant at the injustice being done Blue. Reason an plead as she would, she could not alter her mother's attitud toward the horse, which was "Better to be safe than sorry."

The stallion was neither mean nor tricky in Luis's esti mation but his was the unhappy position of being in th middle. Actually he sided with Andy. Nevertheless he too his orders from Mrs. Bard; thus he had to abide by he decisions.

Only Blue Smoke was neutral, whinnying lonesomely to whoever passed by, his soft brown eyes watching anxiously for his old friend who never came. It was out of the question for the horse to stand day in and day out in a stall yet the ranch work required every minute of Luis's time, so Blue was moved outside to a corral. There he ran loose, unkempt and neglected except for the night and morning hay pitched over the bars. This was the final thorn in Andy's discontent.

"It's not fair to the horse," she stormed. "He's used to good care."

"He's not so bad off," Mrs. Bard demurred. "He eats regularly. The corral's big enough for him to get what exercise he needs. Certainly the weather is warm enough now so he doesn't need shelter. What more could he want?"

"He's lonely and grieving. It's loving he needs, not just food."

"Maybe he doesn't know it, but he's doing a lot better than he has any right to expect."

Whatever leisure Andy had she spent sitting beside the corral to prove to Blue that he was not entirely unloved and alone. Tufts of green grass, carrot tops, any tidbits Andy could get hold of were pushed through the bars into his manger but she kept to the letter of her promise and did not touch Blue.

Days went by with no hopes of breaking the Bar D's deadlock. Andy's brain was not idle while she sat by the corral but scheme and contrive as she would she could find no answer to either puzzle. On her first visit to town she called at the doctor's office to ask whether there had been any medical symptoms that might prove that Pop had died before Blue dragged him. Even that slim lead petered out.

"No, Andy, it's very possible, even probable, but with the two events occurring almost simultaneously it's impossible to say definitely. I'm sorry I can't help you more."

Even a horse knows when he is an outcast. Blue became quiet, even morose, paying little attention to his surroundings except when someone appeared on the footpath from Pop's old cabin. Then for a moment he would act like a wild horse, charging the fence and neighing exultantly, but as soon as the person was identified Blue lost interest. His rations were as generous as ever (except for the grain which his inactivity ruled out) but he was losing weight, and the burnished sheen faded from his coat until he looked like any horse.

"Poor old Blue. I might better have let them shoot you than to have you die of a broken heart. If only we could ride out together you wouldn't grieve so for Pop."

Pop's death seemed to have put a jinx on the ranch, its dude ambitions, everything. As day after day went past with no new reservations Mrs. Bard's anxiety began to show through and she watched eagerly for every mail. She sighed despairingly when one delivery brought only bills.

"Goodness! I'd welcome anything in the way of dudes right now."

She was to regret those rash words before the week was out. Reservations for two weeks were made by telephone from Los Angeles for a family of seven, Mr. and Mrs. J. Barclay Whitcomb and five children, from a toddler of two to a boy of sixteen.

"That stallion is certainly our skeleton in the closet,"
Mrs. Bard fretted. "I wish we had one big enough to hide
him in. I can't draw an easy breath so long as he's around,
but on pain of bread and water for a week—no, a month—
don't one of you dare breathe in front of our guests that
he's a killer."

"*I* certainly shan't," Andy flashed, "because he isn't."

"We've no time for debates now, Andrea," her mother

said crisply. "Just see to it that the Whitcombs' young one
don't get near him."

"Muz, I'm a dude wrangler, not a baby sitter," And
protested. "Can't they watch their own kids?"

"I daresay Mrs. Whitcomb can look after Two and Fou
but the three older ones are up to *you* three to keep tal
on. *And keep them away from that stallion.*"

Saturday morning almost before the long, yellow ca
stopped, the back doors flew open and children swarme
out in every direction. Mrs. Bard's words of welcome wer
scarcely audible in the hubbub. Andy knew a moment c
thankfulness that such clamor would be off in the cottag
by itself at least part of the time but the thought of tw
weeks of it gave her a bad attack of gooseflesh.

"I want to go riding," the eldest, soon identified as
Barclay Whitcomb, III, announced.

"Me too," yelled the second boy, the one called Chucl

"Me too," whooped their sister, Eleanor. "Heigh-ol
Silver, awa-a-a-ay!"

"Me too," echoed the sprite of four.

There was no denying nor even delaying this mass stam
pede, for each was already dressed in blue jeans and nev
boots. Luis was out with the tractor so Andy took her cue

"All right, come along if your folks don't mind. Val an
Jump, you might as well come too," she said casually, gla
that she could call out the reserves.

"Jump—is that your name? What a funny thing to ca
you. Are you jumpy?" Chuck snickered.

Andy held her breath, expecting to see dude blood spille
then and there but her brother came through in the pinch

"I don't think it's funny. I like it."

The other Bards exhaled slowly and gratefully. Andy hastily organized her mob and headed them for the stables. Telling the three Whitcombs to stay by the hitching rack (luckily the senior Whitcombs had had the sense to veto their four-year-old's ambitions) the three Bards haltered six horses and brought them around to be saddled.

"That's a horse?" Jay exclaimed when his was led up to him. "I don't like it. I want to ride that one." Jay pointed to Blue.

"You can't. No one can," Andy said shortly. "Here, up you go. Haven't ridden much, have you, Jay?"

"Sure, I've done lots of riding," the boy bragged, not knowing how thoroughly his awkwardness contradicted his speech.

That was a ride the Bards never forgot. It was more like trying to herd a covey of quail. The horses too thought they had gone to sleep and waked up in a rodeo as the Whitcombs raced and whooped back and forth. Even on the way home in spite of Andy's admonitions their speed never slackened until the Bards' mounts too were worked to a lather trying to keep some semblance of control.

"Every good horseman walks his horse until it's cool," Andy announced firmly back at the stables. "I'll tell you, we'll do it like they do at the racetracks. Everyone off, loosen the cinch a little, like this, and we'll walk around and around in a circle to cool them out. It's sort of 'follow the leader.' Fall in behind me and when I let my horse drink, you let yours take five swallows of water—no more. Come on."

The Whitcombs stepped out smartly but it did not take many circuits until the new boots began to chafe. A few more turns and muscles unused to saddles groaned louder and louder.

"It's really lots easier to walk the horse the last mile in, saves a lot of foot work, but this's kind of fun. They call it 'walking hots' at the tracks," she called over her shoulder with pretended gaiety, silently noting the hobbling Whitcombs.

Jump and Val were with her in spirit and they tramped along beside their horses as if they did it every day. The Bards were forced to grudging admiration for the others' fortitude before Andy pronounced the horses cool enough to turn out. Not a murmur of complaint had the Whitcombs made. If that was the way things were done on a dude ranch they would stick it out, but Andy would have wagered Pop's peck of pennies that after the next ride the horses would come in cool.

"Why do you keep that hayburner around if no one rides him?" Jay inquired when Andy stopped by Blue's corral.

"He's a famous racehorse. Too valuable to get rid of."

Andy, seeing that a stout chain and padlock had appeared on Blue's gate while they were out riding, guessed that her mother had given Luis a storm warning. Otherwise the girl would never have dared to brag about the horse's prowess.

"I'll bet Blue knows where his papers are," Andy mused. "Pop probably talked it all over with him that fatal day, told him he had arranged for his future, told him where he'd put the papers!"

"Hey, wake up! For the tenth time, whose is he?" Jay waved his hands before her eyes.

"Mine." Andy took comfort from the forthright monosyllable though she added a silent "Almost" to herself.

·9·

Blue Sunday

It was a full-time job for everyone to look after all the Whitcombs and keep them happy. For once Mrs. Bard was thankful that there were no other guests to be considered for if Jay wasn't acting like Monte Montana, Chuck was trying to ride a calf, or the toddler had to be snatched from the jaws of danger.

To the Whitcombs themselves, however, who lived in constant turmoil, it was almost too quiet and peaceful in the country. Mr. and Mrs. Whitcomb missed evening entertainment while the younger ones clamored for a rodeo at least once a day. In desperation the Bards connived in secret.

"I suppose we might ask in some friends for a Saturday night of square dancing," Mrs. Bard speculated. "We could have a buffet supper so both dining and living rooms could be ready for the dance."

"Some of the cattle in that last shipment of fatteners aren't fit for much but roping stock," Andy said eagerly. "Let's cull out a few of the worst scrubs and have ourselves a rodeo. We could send out the word to all our local cowboys—some of the best on the coast live right around here. Do you think they'd come, Luis, if we offered a few

prizes as well as turned the entry money back into jack-pots?"

"I don't see why not. Those boys will rope and ride just for the fun of it—and in front of an audience it's that much more fun. If it's all right with you, Mrs. B., I'll spread it around when I go in to the village this afternoon."

"Just tell Gabby Armstrong. He's better'n a party line," Andy giggled.

"Let's see, this is Thursday already. We'll have to work fast, but I can handle the Saturday night dance details, Luis, if you can get ready for our little rodeo on Sunday," Mrs. Bard decided.

Andy, Jump and Val had little to do with the preparations as their time was so completely devoted to riding herd on the younger Whitcombs. Andy would not have thought it possible for them to devise new shenanigans but with prospects of a Wild West Show practically their own Jay and his brothers and sister outdid themselves. By Saturday afternoon Andy's head was reeling, and she breathed a sigh of relief to be rid of her charges at least until morning.

With the prospect of a party she found new strength to bathe and dress in her best shirt and saddle pants. Her old, scuffed boots were beyond restoring to anything approaching style and she glared at them bitterly. One boot off and one boot on, she clumped to her mother's door and rapped.

"Muz, just look at these boots. They're awful!"

"Ummm, they don't look so good but there's lots of wear left in them yet. You look very nice tonight, dear," Mrs. Bard replied absent-mindedly, continuing her own dressing.

"Hey, Muz, you look pretty slick tonight yourself." Andy for once really saw her mother as a pretty woman dressing for a party. "Got a date?" she teased.

"Yes, and right now. The Whitcombs invited a friend up from Los Angeles for the weekend. He's waiting in the living room for me to show him his room. 'Bye now."

Andy couldn't close her mouth in time to answer this airy farewell. She found herself alone in her mother's room waving her battered boot at nothing.

"But, Muz," she wailed after her, "what about my boots? They pinch."

"Where? Your feet or your pride?" A soft laugh took the sting from her mother's reply.

"What's got into her?" Andy wondered while she finished dressing. "She does act like a girl going to a party—her first party too."

Andy soon forgot her mother's strange behavior in her own anticipation. She was amazed and a little flattered to find Jay waiting for her. Without the worry of whether he was going to kill himself or a horse, Andy found his thin, dark face with its curly crown attractive, while his imperious air, no longer a challenge to her own dude wrangler authority, was quite complimentary. Baby Tommy and four-year-old Francis having been put to bed early, the six juniors spread themselves about the porch and, following a systematic clearance of twice-heaped plates, they were ready for the evening.

Mrs. Bard had hired a piano player and fiddler-caller whose discordant tuning-up sounds heightened the festive expectancy. Andy was perhaps more eager than the rest, for the Bards had long been square dance enthusiasts and she had learned to "grand right and left" and "forward and back" to phonograph music.

She secretly hoped that some handsome young stranger would appear for a partner but when at the call "Choose your partners" J. Barclay Whitcomb, III, chose her she accepted with a smile.

"I hope you know what we're supposed to do, Andy. It looks like acrobatics to music."

"Sure, I'll show you. It's fun."

They took their places on the floor with the other couples to be whirled into the fun and excitement of a dance as old, as authentic as a page from a history book. Its steps traced

the course of American pioneers as surely as had the cov
ered wagons that drove westward.

At first Jay was as unwieldy as a water-logged boat, and
he apparently had a talent for doing the wrong thing, bu
Andy coached him with words and none-too-gentle shoves

"For goodness' sakes, listen to what the man's saying
He's telling you what to do!"

"He is! I thought that was just sound effect to confus
us further."

Once Jay's ear tuned itself to the caller's jargon, half
sung, half-spoken, Andy's task grew easier. Through th
maze of dancers Andy caught sight of her mother whose
gay expression and smile as she turned to salute her partne
made Andy miss a step. An idea struggled to take shape bu
the dance went on, her half-formed thought being lost in
fast footwork.

Jay's dogged determination to master the square danc
reminded Andy of his Bar D initiation when they coole
out the horses, for so long as there was strength and contro
in his legs they danced. Lacking the handsome young
stranger she had dreamed of, Andy found Jay a pleasan
substitute and she was sure the musicians' watches wer
wrong when they swung into *Home, Sweet Home*.

It was really midnight, however. The young folks lef
their elders still milling around and after a swift raid on
the kitchen they hurried off to bed, for summer dawn
comes early.

Since Luis and the three Bards were to bring in the cattle
culls as rodeo stock, it was agreed that Jay, Chuck and
Eleanor should go along, not for their help but as the best

possible way to keep them out of trouble. With Luis there to help with the saddling Andy had time for a quick call on Blue who moped in a corner. She thrust him a little grass, all the time showering him with soft talk before she returned to her duties.

"Blue wasn't mean to start with but it'll be a wonder if he doesn't turn mean. Nothing, man or beast, can hold out forever if the world's against him," she mourned to Luis.

"Yeah, I've been thinking that. He's getting more and more morose. That's apt to be a danger signal though he did a funny thing yesterday. Mrs. Whitcomb was walking the baby. When they stopped by the corral the kid waved his arms and googled at Blue who trotted up to the fence with a nicker rumbling in his throat. Soon as they turned away (and I watched until they did) he went back to his sulking corner."

"And sulked," Andy concluded sadly. "Oh, if I could only dream up a trick for pulling a rabbit out of a hat—or a horse out of a corral."

She had little time for dreaming of any kind from there on although with Luis in charge she was spared the worst. Before mounting, he opened the gate into the corral next to Blue's where they intended to drive the stock. Everyone else was horseback and he faced them grimly.

"Now then, kids, when you drive stock you do it quietly and slowly—so slowly that you have to keep checking your horse as it naturally walks faster than a critter. Understand? If you don't want to do it that way, you can get off now, because we aren't going to do any running." He paused to look searchingly at each Whitcomb. "OK, it's a bargain."

The early morning was too freshly beautiful to be rushed through anyway. Sunbeams slanted through the treetops to make rainbows on the dewy grass. A gentle breeze passed smoothly over their faces like running water while every bird tried to outsing its fellows. Nature's beauty was not enough to keep the Whitcombs under control for long, however, and Andy detected mutinous symptoms.

"Let's see who can point first to any object the initial letter of which spells out Whitcomb," she suggested quickly, being psychologist enough to choose their own name to spell. "All's I can think of though that begins with W is 'woc,' that's cow backward."

" 'Water,' " Jay exclaimed cockily, as if the wave of his hand had caused the spring to flow. "Hawk," Jump contributed. "Insect." Andy slapped at a fly to illustrate. "Tree," Val chimed in. "Creek," "Cloud"—the younger Whitcombs vied with each other. "Oak," Andy added. "Mutt." Jay nodded at the Bards' dog over their shouted protests of "Mountain." "Bush," Val finished with a flourish.

"Let's do 'Bard' now," Jay cried. "Bee!" and the others followed his lead.

It was fortunate Andy had hit upon a popular diversion, for the cattle were as far away as they could possibly be and it took a long time to drive them in. Luis kept as watchful an eye on the Whitcombs as on the cattle but thanks to Andy's ingenuity the children behaved themselves.

The stock was not as co-operative. One ornery old steer in particular did not like being taken from its pleasant pasture and pushed around. A set of sharp horns made it look

especially mean. As one break for freedom after another
was thwarted it grew madder and madder. Once when its
escape was blocked it stood spraddle-legged, facing its mas-
ters and jerking its horns suggestively.

"Wow! What it could do to you with those spikes!"
Jump shivered.

"I'm not sure it wouldn't either," Luis said thoughtfully.
"It's a good thing we're getting it out of the herd. It's a bad
influence. Don't anyone dismount—unless you're looking
for a foot race."

The other cattle were getting restless as the old steer's
tactics spread. More than one tail had a quirk in it and
the Bar D folks knew cattle well enough to realize that the
whole bunch was spoiling for trouble. Andy looked long-
ingly toward the open gate at the pasture's end.

"Not too much farther if we can keep 'em moving."

"We'll take it easy-like so's not to stir 'em up any more
than necessary. They'll make a beeline for the gate when
we get them closer," Luis stated.

The old steer grew more and more difficult to handle
until it saw the open gate at last, which looked like sure
escape. It galloped through, the other cattle bunched close
around it, as Luis and his helpers sighed with relief. Only
momentarily, for their eyes widened incredulously as they
followed the cattle's charge. Four-year-old Francis, still in
his pajamas, was standing on the free-swinging inner gate
between the first corral and Blue's.

Startled at being caught in mischief the boy jumped
down, bawling lustily, but on seeing the cattle bearing
down on him his perfunctory howls turned to terrified

screams. Luis spurred and quirted his bay and she sprang forward but too late to swerve the herd that raced straight across the corral toward the boy and the open gate.

A convulsive scramble, less thought than instinct, rolled him under the fence just as the old steer, mad with speed, crashed through the gate to lead the others into Blue's corral. Francis huddled down by the gate post, staring into the forest of red and white legs as they thundered past.

Drawn by Francis's shrieks, Mrs. Bard reached the scene at that moment but her screamed warning was too late. Baby Whitcomb had crawled under the lowest bar into Blue's corral where he sat, sifting dust through his fingers, between the charging cattle that burst through the gate at one end and the excited stallion in the other. The thunder of hoofs diverted his attention from play. Young though he was he knew things were not right. He lurched to his feet only to sprawl out flat a moment later while his bellows were added to the commotion.

Luis and the riders were helpless, for they were behind the cattle, yet only instant action could avert a tragedy. An unmounted person would be powerless to turn the cattle; nevertheless Mrs. Bard raced for the fence.

Until then the cattle had been the greater threat but Mrs. Bard's rush seemed to touch off the stallion. He too lunged toward the terrified child, every plunging hoof an instrument of death. A blue bolt, his charge carried him so close to the baby it was showered with dust and pebbles but the horse passed him, driving straight for the trouble-making leader.

The wily old fellow dodged, almost evading Blue, but quick as a cat the horse sat back on his haunches, spun around and stayed between herd and child. The unexpected

onslaught arrested the cattle's first rush. The stallion followed up mercilessly, wheeling, charging, biting, rushing. He was everywhere but always between the baby and the cattle.

All except the steer were easily discouraged but, mad clear through from the day's indignities, it was determined to work off its anger on that small, convenient target. It dodged, it feinted, but the blue shadow stayed with it.

In one lightning motion Mrs. Bard slipped between the bars and sprinted into the corral. Snatching up the baby, she ran back to the fence. Through the cloud of dust the steer caught the flash of color. Tail in air, it charged, only to find the horse blocking its way again. When this rush was foiled, the steer jerked its horns sideways, tracing a red gash across Blue's side.

Meanwhile Luis had driven the less belligerent cattle back into their own corral. The target in front removed and its mob behind it gone, the old steer began to give ground. Finally it too turned and fled, bawling lonesomely to its fellows.

Mr. and Mrs. Whitcomb, she in a satin negligee and he still struggling into his robe, reached the scene just as Mrs. Bard and Tommy slipped between the corral bars and Andy deposited Francis outside. One swift glance wiped their parents' eyes clear of sleep. Mrs. Whitcomb clutched both children so tightly she seemed about to strangle them while everyone babbled with relief.

One look showed Andy that, though thoroughly frightened, the youngsters were all right before she slipped back into the corral to Blue. She flung her arms around his neck in an attempt to make up for the past weeks' neglect.

"Oh, Blue, you're a real hero—you repaid us with kindness for all the harsh things that have been said and done to you. You even shed your blood to help us. How bad is it, fellow? Let's have a look."

She gently touched his side while she examined the wound, a slit as neat as a knife would make.

"It'll take stitches—several of them—and you may always carry a scar, but it'll be an honorable scar, one you can be proud of."

Finding that the children were unharmed, the others' attention also turned toward the horse and his corral where in the untrampled, near end they could read a story. Bits of hay and grass and tiny footprints mixed and overlaid with hoof marks showed that Blue and the baby had already made friends. Then, tiring of petting the horse, the child had picked out a soft spot for playing sandpile while Blue dawdled near his first real company in weeks.

"Remember, Muz, I've said all along a baby'd be safe with Blue—but you wouldn't believe me!"

"Yes, dear, I admit I was wrong."

"So now I get to ride Blue when I want to? Today— 'Blue Sunday'—or any day?"

"Ye-es, but you'll have to wait for that gash to heal before he can be saddled," Mrs. Bard temporized, finding it difficult to do so abrupt an about-face.

"Shucks, I can ride him bareback, eh, Blue? Pop used to."

"All right, all right. I give up— That way the most he can do is throw you."

"I just phoned the vet, Andy," Luis said, rejoining the group. "He'll be right out to sew up Blue. Said he was coming this afternoon anyway for the rodeo and might as well make it a little earlier."

"Rodeo!" Mr. Whitcomb feverishly clapped his hand to his forehead. "Do we have to have one? I've had all I want today."

"Can't call it off now, Mr. Whitcomb," Luis said matter-of-factly. "The vet surely isn't the only one who planned to come. We'll have to go on with it."

·10·

Fresh Start

The afternoon's rodeo was an anticlimax for the Whitcombs as well as a cruel reminder of the tragedy their negligence might have caused. For everyone else it was a gala time but no one enjoyed it more thoroughly than Andy and Blue. The veterinarian had taken six stitches to draw the cut together while Andy hovered lovingly over the horse, showering him with endearments and tasty morsels although he stood patiently throughout the doctoring.

As the hero of the hour no one could do enough for the roan stallion. Andy gave him his first thorough grooming in a long time. When she touched a particularly ticklish spot he stretched his neck and twitched his upper lip blissfully while Andy brushed the harder.

"Muz, if you don't need me this afternoon, I guess I'll ride Blue to help Luis move the stock around for the different events," the girl said casually after lunch, wanting her horse to be in the limelight where he could receive the admiration he deserved.

"Ride Blue! I should think he ought to have a rest after that workout this morning."

"No, I asked the vet who says it'd be better to keep him moving a while, that he's apt to go lame from such violent exercise after so long a lay-off. If he's just walked around his muscles won't have a chance to tighten up."

"We-e-ll, I suppose it'll be all right." Mother instincts are hard to change as fast as things had happened that morning.

"Now you've got to get over feeling like that about Blue. He *may* have taken a life, though I still don't believe it, but there's no denying he saved one today."

As Blue's story spread that afternoon the roan received all the praise and admiration Andy could have wished for. Only one thing happened to mar her enjoyment.

"Some horse you've got for yourself, Andy," one of the ropers said to her. "If you ever want to get rid of him, give me first choice, will you?"

"Don't worry—I never will," she replied lightly but it set other words buzzing in her head.

"A ward of the court—you cannot sell or otherwise dispose of the animal—" had been the coroner's words. The horse she rode, *her* horse, was not really hers at all unless she could prove it, but for the moment she thrust away the shadow.

When the afternoon's fun was over, Blue was given a brisk rubdown and blanketed lightly before being stabled in his old stall.

"There you are, fellow. Things are back to normal and they'll stay that way—if I can just find your papers." She stroked the roan nose thoughtfully.

"Papers?" Jay who had been helping her looked up curiously.

Andy sketched Blue's story and her dilemma which fascinated him.

"Why, it's as good as a detective story right here. I'll bet I can find them for you in no time."

"Oh, yeah? Let's see you."

His experience in listening to radio mysteries and watching them on television made him feel like an authority so he began his search with unbounded confidence. During the Whitcombs' remaining week at the Bar D nothing was safe from Jay's investigations. He attacked Pop's cabin with such vigor it seemed that not a brick would be left standing, but with no more success than Andy had had.

When it came time for the Whitcombs to leave they almost had to take Jay by force. He had found people he liked, things he liked, in a place where his boundless energy was not always running up against other people's restrictions and prohibitions. He begged his father to let him spend his vacation at the Bar D.

"It's out of the question, son. Have you forgotten we're going to visit your grandmother next month?"

"She'd never miss me out of the mob, Dad. Can't I please stay 'til you get back?"

His mother tried to tease him out of it. "What? Mrs. J. Barclay Whitcomb, Sr., not miss J. B. W., the three! You just don't want to leave Andy."

"Of course I don't. She needs help to find those papers."

Andy could see that Jay was not used to losing arguments, but that one did not go in his favor.

"I'll keep thinking about it, Andy, and write you if I get any brainstorms. Those papers must be here some place and we'll find 'em," he vowed in unwilling farewell.

Despite Andy's uneasiness over proving her rights to Blue, she was so engrossed with the horse himself everything else was pushed to the back of her mind. For several days she was obliged to ride him bareback but it was no hardship since his round, well-muscled back made a comfortable seat.

Before Blue could be saddled again Mrs. Bard made a trip into the city. On her return she called to her daughter who, as usual, was out with the horse.

"Andy, come here a minute. I brought you a present."

"Me, Muz? What?"

"Boots, come and see how you like them. It's a little early but you can call them your birthday present."

Boots, at last! The girl pulled off her old ones, straining and tugging realistically to prove how tight they were. She ripped open the big box and almost reverently took out a shining red boot, appliquéd with white figures, stitched with colored thread.

"Oh, Muz! They're beautiful."

She braced herself to pull on the right boot but it slipped on like a bedroom slipper.

"It's miles too big. We'll have to exchange them." Disappointment over the delay flitted across her face. "I hope they'll have this pattern in a smaller size."

"They have, but I bought them large on purpose, Andrea, insurance that you never get hung up in a stirrup."

"Muz, I thought we had agreed that Blue wasn't really to blame."

Argue and cajole as she would Andy could not get her mother to return the boots. It was large ones or none at all so Andy finally gave in as gracefully as she could.

"Well, thanks heaps, Muz. I guess I can wear heavier socks inside 'em. That way they won't feel so sloppy."

Blue's wound was healing rapidly, proof of his tremendous vitality. Andy had a secret hope which now grew brighter and brighter. The Bar D needed publicizing. She and Blue had shown they were a winning combination on the track. Not many miles nor weeks away there was to be an afternoon of Quarter Horse racing. It all added up, she reasoned, to entering Blue.

She would be riding against seasoned jockeys since there was no ladies' race but her boundless confidence in her horse's speed outweighed whatever misgivings she had.

Andy knew that she would meet her toughest opposition right there at home so before broaching the subject she set about getting Blue back into first class condition.

Every minute she was not needed elsewhere which was a good share of the time because the dude business was so slow, Andy spent with Blue Smoke, riding him up hill and down to harden his muscles. Before he was ready to wear a bulky stock saddle again, Andy used the tiny racing saddle. This gave her a chance to get used to it.

After a few days' practice with the small saddle, Andy rode the horse to a flat strip in a remote section of the ranch. Today she wanted no audience. She dismounted and with a stick drew a line on the dry ground as Pop had done.

"Guess this is what you might consider making a fresh start, Blue."

Remounting, she rode the horse up to the line. Grabbing a generous handful of mane, she leaned forward, counting to "Three" and "Go!" For once she was grateful that Blue didn't snap forward with his usual explosion, for such saddle as she had was little better than no saddle at all. Blue knew what to expect the next time, however, catapulting forward with such force Andy wobbled wildly on his back.

"Zowie! That'd look terrible on a track, Blue. You're OK but I need plenty of practice. Let's try it again," she said breathlessly after stopping his rush.

Doggedly she turned the stallion and rode back to the improvised starting line, but he contrarily whirled to face in the opposite direction despite her best efforts to straighten him out. Once when he was headed almost right Andy crouched over his neck, knees bent and head low, only to snap suddenly erect.

"Think you're smart, don't you?"

No one but Jump could pack so much sarcasm into so few words. He rode out of a nearby thicket.

"You, huh! No wonder I couldn't make Blue face the other way. He knew you and old Sam were there all the time." Andy knew there was no hiding her intentions. She faced her brother blandly. "What's on your mind?"

"Nuthin much. Just finding out what's on your mind. Wait'll Muz hears about this."

" 'Wait' is the word for it, Jump. I'm getting him in shape for the Quarter Horse races and if I have him all ready to run I hope she'll let me ride him. You know as well as I do that the Bar D needs some advertising, so just keep quiet a few more days, huh?"

"We-ell, maybe I could if you could see things my way." Jump was elaborately casual.

"Such as?" Andy held her breath. What was he up to?

"Such-as-letting-me-ride-him-once." The boy's words fell over each other with haste.

"Why, sure. You didn't have to resort to blackmail; I'd have let you before if you'd asked me. First though, help me with a few more starts. Boy, they're sure tricky to get the hang of."

One or two more starts were enough for that day but Andy was still dissatisfied with her performance. It was much more difficult, she found, to synchronize with another's counting so she was glad that Jump had appeared.

What a disgrace it would be to be left flat-footed at th
start.

"Your turn now, Jump. Shall we change saddles too?"

"No need. If you can ride that speck, so can I."

Jump scrambled up, settling himself as best he coul
while Andy mounted Sam. They set off toward home b
either the practice starts or the strange rider had unsettle
the usually placid stallion's nerves. He pranced and jigge
sideways, first one way, then the other, while Jump stro
to look at home on the little saddle.

"A canter might settle him down a little," Andy sug
gested. "Want to try?"

At Jump's nod she swung Sam into a lope but Blu
thought it was a race and shot ahead, his rider clinging de
perately to whatever holds he could get.

"Rein him around, Jump. Turn him back this way.
Andy yelled after him.

Knowing there was no use trying to help with poke
Sam, she pulled him to a halt. Blue lost interest fast with
out another horse to race against, allowing himself to b
circled back to the others. Jump recovered his poise raj
idly on the return but he had had enough.

"Here's your horse. Thanks for the ride." He grinne
as they again changed mounts.

Evidence of Blue's return to prime condition was show
on his coat where, in spite of his exertions, there wa
scarcely a hair out of place. Nevertheless, like good horse
men they walked the horses all the way home.

"Do you honestly think, Andy," Jump finally asked
"that you can get Muz to let you ride Blue in a real race?

"I don't know, Jump, but I'm sure going to try."

Andy hadn't long to wait and during the intervening days she was tireless in perfecting Blue's training. Although the cut on Blue's side was completely healed she greased it religiously to prevent, if at all possible, any scarring, and she spent just about every waking minute with the horse. Together they rode back and forth across the Bar D's ranges and hills until she felt she knew every blade of grass by sight.

With entries closing on a Friday, Andy set her own deadline for Thursday to allow herself a little extra time in order that she would not have to press her mother for an immediate answer. As it turned out, however, her strategy was useless, for Mrs. Bard replied with an emphatic "No!" to Andy's first suggestion. Neither time nor talk could alter it.

"But, Muz, he can win. I know he can. And think of the publicity."

"Publicity be hanged," her mother said shortly. "I don't think we're in such bad shape that I need to risk your neck for advertising purposes."

"Blue wouldn't—" Andy began hotly but her mother interrupted her.

"Riding in a race it wouldn't be just Blue. There are other horses and other riders, none of them as concerned about your neck as I am. If you were riding just any old plug it might be different but Blue is a real threat so every jockey in the race would know Blue was the horse to beat. They might not be too careful in the way they went about

it either. Today, tomorrow, next year, always, the answ
is 'No.' You can *not* ride Blue against professionals."

"He's fit, Muz. He could leave 'em all behind so nobo
could touch us."

"You all start together, don't you? Anything could ha
pen. What about that start in the ladies' race when y
were nearly knocked down? If he's fit and ready to go, I
rather pay for a jockey myself than have you ride him."

This was something Andy had never thought of. All h
dreams and plans had been for her and Blue together. Sl
considered this new angle in silence. After all, Pop hir
self had gotten jockeys when he could.

"Do you think we could still get a good one, Luis?"

"Um-m, probably. You know a lot of the Quarter Hor
owners bring their own boys. I haven't heard that Robb
Gates has a full card."

"Is he a good boy? And honest?"

"Yes, and again yes."

Andy knew when she was beaten. If she and Blue cou
not race together, he might still run and win, with the B
D profiting just as much.

"All right, let's see if we can get him. I'll pay you bac
Muz, out of Blue's winnings."

·11·

"No Next Time"

Between posting her entry and the day of the race Andy was more nervous than if she had been slated to ride the horse herself. She had entered Blue in the full quarter-mile run, scorning the short dashes as unworthy of his stamina, for short though a quarter mile seems, she knew that covering the distance at full speed was enough to separate the horses from the nags.

Only Andy, Luis and Jump were going to the races. "You'll tell us all about it anyway, dear," her mother chided playfully, "so I'm sure that will be just as good." Andy was very solemn with her new owner-trainer responsibilities as she checked off the gear to be taken along.

Blue was to run in the sixth race but since Robbie Gates would be busy, once the program started, riding one horse after another, they met with him before the first race. Andy liked his looks the minute she saw him, feeling at once that Blue would be in capable hands. She was surer than ever when he brought home the winners of the first and third races.

When Robbie rode out for the fifth, Andy and Luis were busy with the stallion. They heard the familiar roar that signaled the start but before it died away it swelled

into one, sharp excited cry that chopped off to comple
silence. After one heart-stopping second the muffled cha
ter of the loudspeaker filled the pause until the spectato
caught their breaths and babbled excitedly.

Ordinarily their curiosity would have been enough
send Andy or Luis out to see what was going on, but f
the moment getting Blue ready for his race was more in
portant. Within seconds Jump came tearing back to t
stables.

"Andy! Luis! There was a big mix-up when the hors
broke. Robbie was thrown and they're taking him away
an ambulance."

"Robbie? How horrible! Was he hurt bad? How'd
happen?" both exclaimed together, but one thought so
flashed into sharp focus.

"What'll we do for a rider?"

Luis went out to scout around in search of a replaceme
for Robbie, Jump going too in preference to merely wa
ing around with Andy and Blue. Andy's spirits were
low as they had been high a few minutes earlier when s
had been on tiptoe with the excitement of saddling h
horse for a race.

"Blue, we have plenty of luck—but all of it seems to
bad. Are you the black cat in the partnership, or am I?

She leaned against his shoulder and pressed her che
against his shiny neck. He stood immobile but as the silen
grew longer he turned his head to investigate.

"All right, I take it back. You're not the bad luck. We
I'm not either. We'll make out some way. Luis'll probab
find somebody right off."

Her faith in the foreman's ability was instantly rewarded when a strange voice sounded at her shoulder.

"A man told me you need a jockey for the next race."

Andy spun around. A wiry, little man with a young-old look on his face stood before her. For one heartbeat Andy wished Luis had found someone as nice as Robbie but this thought was swept away by the relief flooding through her. Blue could run after all.

"Yes, we do, and right now. You look like you've had lots of experience."

"Yes, I have, ma'am. Been riding for years."

Luis and Jump appeared in the doorway and Andy called out happily.

"Here's our man, Luis. You finish the arrangements. As for orders"—she turned to the jockey—"just get out in front and stay there. He's got what it takes."

Time was running out. Already the loudspeaker was calling horses to the track for the sixth race. Luis gave the new jockey, Bill Sherwin, a leg up, and the business details were settled while Luis accompanied Blue and his rider to the track gate.

"Hey," Andy called suddenly, running after them. "Better give me your bat. You don't need one for Blue."

"That's all right. I feel better carrying one. I won't use it."

Sherwin just had time to warm up the horse before all riders were called to the post. Already Andy could tell Blue did not like his rider. The horse tossed his head fretfully, danced sideways as he had with Jump and instead of answering to the bit he gave with his neck rather than his body. Andy saw that the feeling was mutual. Sherwin was getting more and more angry at his mount.

If she could, Andy would have rushed to the starting line to pull her horse out but it was too late for second-guessing. Her hands clenched into white-knuckled fists. Maybe it would be all right.

All horses finally entered the starting gate but Blue was sulky. He liked nothing about the proceedings and plainly showed it. The doors snapped open; the line of horses sprang forward. All but Blue, for instead of his charging-lion spring he loped out casually, falling in behind the other horses that strung out along the rail.

Blue ran easily with no suggestion of the speed he possessed. Sherwin rode him with everything he had but to no avail and the pack pulled away rapidly. Anger and impatience with the horse fused to produce a swift reaction in Sherwin. Andy saw his whip arm flash up and down several times. Blue quit cold. He had had enough so he swerved to turn back toward the stables.

This caught Sherwin off balance and he nose-dived off the left shoulder. A convulsive grab around Blue's neck righted the falling jockey, enabling him to land standing up beside the now motionless horse.

Again the Bar D name was on every lip but for a different reason. Andy couldn't get loaded up to leave fast enough. Inglorious though Blue's race had been the jockey still had to be paid which, in addition to entry money, added up to an expensive day. The bitterest part by far,

however, was having made the ranch a laughingstock for everyone.

The girl slumped in the pick-up's seat on the homeward trip, her thoughts black and hopeless.

"Don't mind, Andy." Jump tried to comfort her. "Next time will be different."

"There ain't gonna be no next time." The whimsical phrase did not conceal her underlying bitterness.

"Why not?" Her brother was no more surprised than Luis at this development.

"Because it's too much of a gamble. If Muz would let me ride Blue, I'd at least feel sure I could get the most out

of him, but depending on hired jocks, not knowing h
they'll get along with Blue, hoping they'll give him an h
est ride—it isn't worth it."

"I guess Bill Sherwin was honest enough," Luis put
"but stallions can be mighty opinionated. Between Bl
not liking him to start with and his going to the whip wl
you told him not to, he might as well have been crooke

"I've been wondering whether he was honest and stu
or dishonest and smart enough to make himself look s
pid," Andy mused. "I didn't like his looks much. In fact
she unburdened her final grievance with a rush—"if y
hadn't picked him out, Luis, I don't think I'd have tal
him."

"I picked him out? I!" Luis exclaimed in an injured to
"Why, you had him practically on the horse before Ju
and I got there."

"Sure, but didn't you send him? He said 'a man t
him.' "

"I did not. I was coming back to say I guessed we'd h
to scratch Blue from the race."

It took an instant for them to realize that each thou
the other had hired Sherwin to ride the stallion. Then
day's disappointments evaporated before the warmth
their laughter.

"There now, you see what I mean about all the thi
that can go wrong? Anyway, Blue's racing comeback
tempt and his re-retirement are practically simultane(
From now on anything he does will be something we
do together, if it's just herding cattle or dudes on
Bar D."

Andy put on a gay face in telling her mother and Val about the day's difficulties, her conclusion that no form of racing was for her and Blue. Alone in her room, however, she dropped her cheerful pose, wondering gloomily what was the use of having so superior a horse if he did no more than their old ranch horses could do. She had all the sensations of a speedboat owner with nothing but a pond to wet its hull in.

Miserable days followed for Andy, beset by the twin riddles of Blue's lost papers and how to capitalize on his abilities for Bar D publicity. Racing him to fame and fortune had seemed the perfect way to advertise the ranch as "Home of Blue Smoke." Andy was discouraged but not defeated. She turned and twisted the problem about much as one handles a mechanical puzzle, trying first one possibility, then another.

To her first perplexity Blue remained aloof but he unwittingly answered the second, thereby launching the two of them into a new, absorbing activity. Together they had ridden over mile after mile of the Bar D's range while Andy pondered her problems, and whenever any cattle were in sight Blue edged nearer to them.

One bright morning when Andy and Blue were roving the pastures they came across some of their first rodeo stock although the cranky steer had long since gone to market. Andy stroked the blue neck to congratulate him anew.

"You've the instincts of a stock horse all right, boy. What a classy cutter you were out there all by yourself. Hey, a cutting horse! I wonder—?"

In real ranch work cutting horses are highly valued spe-
cialists, Andy knew, often being reserved for nothing but
the business of separating cattle from the main herd, such
as all the yearling heifers, or cows without calves. She
knew too that rodeo and horseshow classes simulating actual ranch conditions for these star performers were catching the public's fancy the country over. Best of all, she and
Blue could do it as a team, for girls as well as men rode in
these cutting contests.

"Home of Blue Smoke" would have real significance if
he could break into this upper bracket of stock horses.
Andy's thoughts whirled into star bursts from the impact
of so inspired an idea.

"You must have been born with plenty of cow sense,
Blue," she mused aloud, "or you'd never have been able to
handle that ornery steer like you did. More than likely Pop
worked cattle with you before you raced. I know you have
a terrific burst of speed, you're nimble and light-footed as
a goat—so let's put 'em all together and see if it makes you
a cutting horse."

Andy's voice had grown stronger with every listed at-
tribute. She banged her closed fist on the pommel so resolutely any observer would have known she had reached
some momentous decision. As though this action tore away
a veil from the future she glimpsed the weeks and months
of hard work ahead. Almost, her heart grew faint. Perhaps
it would be better to enjoy the horse as he was rather
than try to fashion a whole new career for themselves.

This impulse lasted only a short time. Instead of continuing their jaunt she turned Blue toward home. Luis sub-

scribed to several horse magazines that periodically carried cutting horse articles and now Andy wanted to read them without a moment's delay. That brought up the question, How much of her new scheme should she tell?

Nothing, was her first impulse, but cooler consideration showed that complete secrecy was not possible for long. While at first she might practice secretly somewhere in the pasture, as Blue improved they would need smaller quarters and a few head of stock to work with. Then too, after cutting an animal out of the herd the horse needs another rider to haze the critter back toward him. In an actual contest this hazer, or turn-back man, is generally another contestant but Andy knew she would need such a helper on horseback.

"No use saying anything about our ambitions though until I get some idea of how you like the work, Blue. If you don't, we might just as well quit now because cutting cattle is something you have to have your heart as well as your hoofs in."

Andy struggled to recall all the cutting contests she had seen in shows and rodeos only to realize that in reality they told her little. She needed to know how the horses' instinctive ability was encouraged and directed to make them topnotch cutters. As soon as Blue had been put up, Andy borrowed a stack of magazines from Luis and hurried to her room where she and the magazines were soon strewn across the bed. Hearing footsteps pause at the doorway she looked up to see her mother staring at her with a worried look.

"What's the matter, Andrea? You don't feel sick, ¿
you?"

"Of course not, Muz. Never felt better in my lif
Why?"

"Coming in so early on a perfectly beautiful day. I
go for a ride myself if I didn't have so much to do. The
you must be up to something."

"Me, Muz? You must be sick yourself—you're imaginiɪ
things."

"Oh, no. I haven't seen such a glint in your eyes
weeks. And now, seeing that baby-eyed stare, I'm sure ¢
it. I suppose you're teaching Blue to fly."

"He knows how already," Andy chortled happily.
just thought it'd be fun to do a little reading."

"As unlikely a story as I've ever heard," Mrs. Bard gru
bled as she retreated down the hall.

One after another, the magazines were sorted into tv
piles, one for copies with something about cutting hors
even if only a picture of a famous horse that sold for
fabulous price, the other for dead wood. One or two arɪ
cles were gold mines of information.

"Start your colt slow," she reviewed aloud. "Five or tɪ
minutes a day are enough at first—work him alone on jᵾ
one animal along a fence—*always* turn the horse's head t
ward the critter."

"Well, that sounds simple enough. I can at least try."

The more she read about cutting horses the more tailc
made the sport seemed for Blue and herself to do as a teaɪ
Another article was devoted entirely to girls who ro
their own cutting horses. Andy could almost see her pɪ

ture there too, mounted on Blue and holding some valuable trophy they had just won.

"Blue Smoke, owned and ridden by Andy Bard of the Bar D, after their sensational win at—"

Andy was hypnotized by her own words, but somewhere a jarring note marred her happiness. There it was.

"*Owned* by Andy Bard."

Well, that was true, wasn't it? She couldn't produce the proof that very minute but surely, surely, she would soon fathom the mystery.

·12·

Finger Exercises

Riding out on Blue the next morning Andy tried to rec[…]
everything Pop had ever told her about Blue's life bef[…]
he became a racehorse. He was born and raised on t[…]
ranch where Pop had worked for several years (thou[…]
if he had ever used its name she had forgotten). There P[…]
had broken him and started his education as a stock hor[…]
for it was in pitting Blue against other cowboys' horses[…]
had discovered what a burst of speed the roan had.

With her new interest Andy was astonished that s[…]
had been so preoccupied with Blue's speed and starts s[…]
had never put him through a figure eight. This basic exe[…]
cise for stock horses, two circles in opposite directic[…]
changing leads at the intersection, tests in one maneuv[…]
the horse's suppleness, balance and lightness on the reins t[…]
gether with his ability to change leads in stride as requir[…]
when following a fast-moving steer.

Despite her eagerness, she waited until Blue had walk[…]
the first mile to try him out. Then as soon as they reach[…]
soft footing she shook him into a lope. First they cut[…]
circle for the top of the eight. Coming back to its wai[…]
she threw Blue onto his other lead to circle the oppos[…]
way.

"Good enough, fellow. Not quite as smooth as the show horses but I can see you know what it's all about. Now let's see how you do at that small circle we read about."

Again she sent him into a canter but held him in one circle, around and around and around, trying to cut it smaller each time. At first he did very well but as the loops grew tighter he tried to swing his rump toward the outside.

"It'll take practice before you can work on a dime and give me five cents change, Blue. Just remember, you've got to learn to turn on your hindquarters or we're licked before we start. All right, let's try it easy on the other lead."

It was all Andy could do to restrain her eagerness whe
they rode past some stock on the way home but her com
mon or horse sense warned her against starting Blue c
cattle before his basic training was complete. The racin
saddle stayed on its peg in the tackroom while Andy
stock saddle looked shiny and ridden once again, but sh
continued to use Blue's own bridle with the snaffle bit.

Andy concentrated on the small circle and she was de
lighted at Blue's response, for as the days went by the ci
cles grew smaller and smaller. Figure eights, to a lesse
degree, were interspersed in the training routine, the abilit
to change leads as often and as rapidly as required bein
fundamental in any cow work.

"Pop really taught you your ABC's, Blue, and they'r
coming back to you so fast you'll soon be down to you
XYZ's. I'm sure glad I'm not having to start from scratc
to make a cutting horse out of a racehorse. All you reall
need is a refresher course in fundamentals."

After a few weeks of reviewing his footwork Andy
could see real progress. The circles had grown tight, s
tight that as Andy looked down one day after pulling u
in the center she tingled with gooseflesh. There, in the dir
lay positive proof of Blue's handiness, for his hoofprint
had actually cut two circles, the inner one made by h
back feet, the outer cut by his fore feet as they range
around his hindquarters.

"Oh, Blue, you're my wonderful guy. I'll bet after
while you really could canter in such a tight loop you
hindquarters would stay on the same spot. We'll jump th
gun this weekend though and start you on cattle easy, bu

we'll keep working on these 'finger exercises' to keep you on your toes."

The girl's confidence had ebbed somewhat by Saturday morning when she and Blue were outward bound on their first cattle lesson. Since first deciding that Blue would make a good cutting horse Andy had digested so many articles from magazines and books, talked to so many cowboys and would-be horse trainers, her head was a jumble of phrases. She was smart enough to understand that she had undoubtedly been given as much well-meant misinformation as genuine help and that it was up to her to sort it out, adapt what she could to her own horse and his personality, throwing the rest away.

Any horse trainer knows that what will work with one horse fails miserably on another. Had anyone asked Andy that morning what her plan was she would have had to admit she herself did not know, except that she was going to do something.

"Cow sense" or "cow savvy" were mentioned as frequently as anything so she rode Blue toward the first cattle she found. The animals watched curiously as horse and rider approached them at a tangent, then veered off just a little to circle the group. Twice they rode around the steers before she reined Blue directly into them.

Voice and rein quieted the horse as, reaching the bunched animals, Andy eased Blue among them. This loosened them up and the girl was content to merely ride through with as little commotion as possible. Blue stepped softly as if he understood his rider's intention. They emerged on the far side leaving only a few eddies behind.

"Good boy, Blue. That's taking it easy all right.
important too. Got to cut your cow brute out of the
without spooking all the others, or the judges'll spank.

That bunch left behind, they rode on, Andy on
look-out for a lone animal that she might work alor
fence, but cattle are gregarious creatures not given to
tude. She sighted several apparent singles but closer
proach always sent them scurrying back to their fell
Reaching the Bar D's farthest line, Andy was about to
up.

"Jiminy, Blue, maybe we'll have to admit to our cr
ambitions if we're to have anything to work on. Can't n
a cutting horse of you unless there's something to cut.

She reined in and sat there a minute while she scan
the open bottom lands and tree-dotted slopes. Her h
jumped to see, far off to one side, the perfect set-up
former Bar D owner had long ago built a holding cc
at this most distant corner in order to save the time
trouble of driving cattle in to the main corrals. Luis n
used it, however, leaving the bars down, in order that e
that small patch of feed might not be wasted.

Some cattle stood under a nearby live oak but inside
a fat, logy steer grazing with the industry that sho
where his beef came from.

"Who said we were unlucky, Blue? We couldn't h
worked out a better set-up if we'd been trying."

Andy loped Blue up to the gate where, dismounting,
pulled it shut with the three of them—steer, horse and ri
—inside. She remounted and turned Blue toward the st
that watched them uneasily. At their approach it lumbe

clumsily along while Andy rode Blue parallel ten or twelve feet out. Watching the steer intently, the horse soon pulled abreast of it.

At this the animal doubled back to change directions. Andy likewise turned Blue around, his head always toward the steer, and the pattern was repeated. She held the reins as lightly as sewing silk so she could not be sure, when Blue again doubled after the steer, whether he did it without reining.

Blue acted so pleased with himself over his achievement Andy wisely decided that was time to end the first lesson. After dismounting she petted and praised her horse extravagantly, then remounted and rode away, leaving the steer to ponder the strange ways of horses and humans.

"You did just fine, Bluesy. You're a natural cutter or I'm a wall-eyed pike. But there's one thing I know for certain: we can't always count on such a lucky deal so we're going to have to confide in the others pretty quick."

The staccato hoofbeats of his short, Quarter Horse stride drummed out background music while Andy considered her next move. She slapped his strong neck approvingly each time his alert ears pointed out a group of cattle.

"Doggone it, Blue! I hate to give everything away until your ability is more than just a gleam in our eyes. Guess there's no other way though if you're to have all the advantages."

Before Andy reached the home corrals, however, her mind was wiped clean of cutting and everything connected with it. At a distance she spotted a strange car and a man

talking with Luis. When she came up to them she halt
Blue.

"Andy, this is Mr.—Mr. Stone from the County Admi-
istrator's Office."

She acknowledged the introduction by a nod of her he
but the only words she could frame were an echo of Lui

"From the County Administrator's?"

"Yes, ma'am. I just dropped by to check on the ho
and to make sure he's all right. We thought perhaps y
could show us his papers by now."

For an instant Andy was too weak with relief to spe
but Luis filled in.

"No, we haven't been able to locate them just yet b
any day now we hope to, eh, Andy?"

"Yes, yes, that's right. Any day now. Meanwhile I g
to keep Blue?"

"Oh, sure. I can see that he's getting good care and i
asmuch as he's a ward of the court that's what concerns
most—so long as there's no contested action. Well, I'll st
in again next time I'm in the valley."

"Yes, do that. We'll likely have the papers by ther
Andy said cheerily with a confidence she was far fro
feeling.

Suppertime discussion that night centered once more
the mystery and even Jump's brow was furrowed wi
intense thought.

"You guys never did find his wallet, did you? Well,
you can't find the papers either, Pop probably had the tv
together—"

"But he'd never hide his wallet!" Andy objected.

"Don't hurry me—I was going to say that probably the wallet fell out of his pocket when he was dragged by Blue."

"Jump, you show signs of intelligence. You're even inspired. Is it still light enough—no," she admitted after a quick glance toward the window. "I'll have to wait 'til tomorrow. Oh, if we'd only thought of that a long time ago while Blue's tracks were still fresh. It's a long chance but it might come through," Andy cried with mounting excitement.

"I'll help you look," Val offered. "I'm good at finding things for Muz."

"Me, too," Jump chimed in. "Betcha I find it."

"If you do, I'll give you a juicy kiss," his older sister caroled.

"You do and I'll throw it away again!"

The Bards, for Muz too elected to take a holiday next day, rode out to look for the bit of leather. Four abreast, they rode along slowly, scanning the ground so intently they had to stop from time to time to rest their eyes.

Once or twice one or another got off for a closer look at something which always turned out to be a false hope.

"Looks like we're wasting our time," Mrs. Bard finally said. "Seems as if we'd have found it if it's to be found."

"It's here, Muz, I just know it is."

Once more the four lined up abreast and rode forward. Andy kept seeing the wallet, only to have it become a dark stone, a piece of bark, anything but the object she sought.

When she did see it, she was too stunned for more than a strangled "Oh!" but the others understood. Andy jumped off to pick the stained, faded billfold out of the grass and dirt. She handed it to her mother to open but hope was already fading. Her fingers told her that nothing as flat and light as that fold of leather could contain the pot of gold at the end of her rainbow.

"No luck, Andrea," her mother said gently. "This is all that's in it."

She held out three one-dollar bills, a little silver, a two-dollar pari-mutuel ticket, a sales slip for two pairs of socks with a shopping list scrawled in pencil on the back, and a penny scales card. "Your weight is 127," it said on one side. On the reverse was his fortune: "You were born under a lucky star, for good health, good friends are yours and you will never be in want."

"Poor Pop. He must have kept that for a laugh," Andy said soberly. "Well, that's that. No papers, but keep thinking, Jump. Something's got to work out. Guess I'll go for a real ride now. Want to come, kids?"

Both the younger children would have been determined to go along had she not asked them but her invitation changed their outlook. They voted to ride back with their mother when Andy turned Blue's head toward the upper pasture. The wind had risen a little and the whispering oaks seemed to be talking to her but in a foreign tongue.

Nothing would go right. Twice her hat blew off. Blue seemed to be either willful or stupid when she tried to cut circles and figure eights. The cattle too were in league against her and not a straggler was to be found. At last Andy realized that the fault was hers so she turned toward home. She found no pleasure there either and moped around like a sick kitten.

By evening her inborn optimism was asserting itself again. She told herself that the situation was no worse than it had been all along. It had, in fact, improved, for now that she knew for certain the papers had not been lost with Pop's billfold, the possibilities had narrowed by one. Her nervous tension gradually eased. As it did she remembered her decision to disclose her new ambition for Blue. The time was right, she knew, when her mother and Luis dawdled over their second cups of coffee.

"Muz, you remember that gleam in my eye a while ago? You *were* right. I was cooking up a scheme and I think it's a dandy, but from here on I'll need help."

Andy had the undivided attention of everyone at the table. Even the dog stared at her intently. She plunged on.

"I think Blue will make a top-notch cutting horse. He's got everything. We've done all the dry work we can and now he needs stock to work on. I was wondering whether Luis could maybe spare us three or four head for practice?"

Andy's sparkling eyes continued to plead her cause after she finished speaking. Luis's approval was instantaneous.

"Say, that is a smart idea, Andy. Why didn't I ever think of it? Blue really ought to make a good 'carving' horse. He *does* have everything. How much have you done with him so far?"

Andy recounted Blue's early work and his progress, and concluded with, "Why, if he hadn't done anything more than keep that steer away from the Whitcomb baby I'd have been willing to gamble on him. He's a natural born

cutting horse, he is, so can't we have a few old scrubs, Mu
huh, please?"

"If you'd stop talking long enough for me to get a wor
in edgeways, I'd tell you it's all right with me if Luis ca
pick out a few that aren't all fattened for market."

Her mother's crisp accents were tinged with irony. Th
girl's eyes turned back to Luis, like a dog's that watches
piece of meat being passed from plate to mouth.

"Likely I can," the foreman agreed. "Probably some o
of that same shipment the old steer came in. That's the la
bunch I buy from that outfit. I still think they stuck in
bunch of ringers on me. The ones I looked at before
agreed to buy weren't the leggy, slab-sided critters w
received. Four enough?"

"Promise me, Andrea, you won't do anything reckless o
foolish, though I must say I'm vastly relieved to hear wha
your plan is. It sounds safe as anything—probably safer tha
just whooping around the hills horseback."

"I promise, Muz. Cutting's really very safe—and cuttin
horse riders can hang on to the horn without any penaltie
Some of the best riders do too! Oh, joy! I can hardly wa
to start Blue on his own cattle."

·13·

Black and Blue

As soon as Luis could arrange it, but not soon enough for an impatient Andy, he and the three Bards rode off the next morning to pick out the four steers for Blue's homework assignment. The first cattle they found were in too good condition to be chivvied around, but several of the low-grade lot were running in the second bunch. Luis drew rein while he and Andy sat their motionless horses to decide which ones to cut out.

"Andy, how about that lanky one with the freckled face?" Luis asked.

"OK, and that bald-faced one there on the far side."

"And that spattered-all-over one," Val piped up.

"That one over there"—Luis pointed to one whose lop ears and shoulder hump suggested Brahma blood—"would probably give you more action than the others. Want him or might he be too fast at first?"

"He'd be fine, I think. We'll be working just one at a time to begin with so it won't hurt if he's pretty quick on his feet. And he can serve as a yardstick as to how well Blue's doing."

"That's the four then. Now all we have to do is cut 'em out and get 'em home. Want to try it?"

"Thanks, no. There're too many and that might confu[...]
Blue. You cut and we kids'll hold—unless Jump wants [...]
cut one out?" She looked at her brother.

"Don't mind if I do," he agreed cockily. "I'll bet o[...]
Sam's a better cutting horse now than Blue."

"*Now* maybe, but wait'll you see how Blue improves[...]

Luis separated Freckles from the herd, driving him [...]
one side where Andy and Val worked busily to hold hi[...]
until Baldy joined them. Jump nosed Sam into the he[...]
after Spatter but he turned out to be a wily one and co[...]
tinually hid behind the others for protection. Jump's p[...]
tience was no longer than his nose. He charged after t[...]
steer like an avenging angel, scattering cattle right and lef[...]

"Take it easy," Andy yelled. "You're supposed to spi[...]
a critter out without its knowing what's happening. T[...]
judges'd mark you out of the running after one whingdin[...]
like that."

"He had it coming," Jump growled.

"Yeah, and you've got him going—away," Andy laughed agreement. "Work him easy."

Meanwhile Luis had caught the Brahma on the herd's fringe and worked him over to the cut by the time Jump had convinced the recalcitrant Spatter that he too must go. Starting them toward the home corrals was easy enough with four riders to four steers. Andy and Blue rode a flank position. The drive was a complete success for her when the roan nipped a straggler on the rump.

"How d'ya like that, Luis? I guess the old boy has cow savvy all right—and he'll take no nonsense or lollygaggin' from the critters either."

The cattle were turned into the small pasture to be readily available for Blue's lessons. That night before Andy's light was turned out she reread and reviewed all the best articles on cutting horses. This so whipped up her enthusiasm that each hour seemed a day until she and Blue were together again.

Horseback once more she gathered the cattle from the small pasture, shutting them in the corral while she happily took Blue out to limber him up. They walked their warm-up mile before Andy loped Blue into the small circles one way and then the other, each time they changed direction turning his head outward around himself.

"That ought to 'get the oil running,' as Jump would say, Blue. Now for a critter—just one at a time is the system at first. That way he can't really get away far enough to discourage you."

She opened the gate into Blue's corral and drove three

steers in there, leaving Freckles behind for their first guinea pig. He walked along the fence that separated him from the others, Andy and Blue doing likewise a few feet nearer the center. Halfway down the fence Freckles turned and trotted back but Andy calmly checked Blue's impulse to trot.

"Easy does it, boy. We'll get there at a walk."

Twice the steer went down and back, Blue acting like his disconnected shadow, but the third time Freckles was thoroughly annoyed. He wanted to get back to the other end closer to his companions. He made a break for it.

"Here's where we open up, Blue!" Wheeling him toward the center of the arena, Andy kicked him out. The horse welcomed a chance to run and he fairly flew. Just past the still-galloping steer Andy reined up and, turning, cut him off as neat as a knife. Freckles changed his plans abruptly and walked back like a sullen convict.

"That's the stuff." Andy slapped the blue neck happily. "That's showing him who's boss around here."

Freckles seemed to resent her words. He stopped and stood at right angles to the fence, daring them to make a move. Blue halted of his own accord to face the steer across the intervening space, neck and head outstretched, his ears tight to his head with displeasure. His hoofs were motionless but Andy felt the quiver of his tensing muscles that spun him on his haunches the very instant Freckles broke. Blue turned him back once more before he was well started.

"Attaboy, Blue! That's reading his mind—and you did it ninety-nine per cent on your own. Here's the place to stop for today. I can tell you're pretty well pleased with yourself."

She dismounted to show that the session was over. After returning the cattle to their small pasture, Andy rode Blue along the upper trail before calling it a day.

Baldy received the nod for Blue's lesson the next day and, while slower, the steer behaved much as Freckles had. Spatter, however, when his turn came had a somewhat different style, doing more dodging than the first two. This suited Andy fine. Cutting horses must be as light on their feet as champion boxers, and dodging and weaving develop it. The Brahma was a disappointment, however, as his only idea was to run, yet it was too soon for fast work except when a steer broke away.

"We'll just leave him alone until you're farther along, old boy. Then we'll show Mr. Steer a thing or two."

Time blurred happily for the busy girl. Blue's promise was rapidly becoming reality when school bells tolled the end of summer. In a subdued sort of way Andy was glad to see her friends again and to exchange vacation news (hers had been exciting enough for a stay-at-home summer) and new classes and teachers were a challenge, but nothing could disguise the fact that Blue's schooling was now secondary to hers.

Andy's real day began after she had jumped off the school bus at the ranch gate, made a whirlwind clothes change and hurried to the corrals. She was most careful not to let her hurry creep over into her horse training, however, and acted as if she had all day for that task.

The first Friday evening after school had started Andy

lingered over Blue's grooming and stabling, the better to
savor the prospect of the weekend ahead. She was filled
with a quiet satisfaction at his ability. A car whirred up
the driveway but Andy paid little attention until door
banged and she heard a familiar racket. Without seeing the
canary-colored car she knew the Whitcombs were back
and felt a sudden warmth which belied her "Them again!"
exclamation as she hurried toward the house.

Mrs. Bard and the senior Whitcombs greeted each other
warmly and, known dangers being less frightening than unknown, the younger Whitcombs' commotion was less ter-
rifying than the first time. Instead of being the ringleader
Jay stood still looking around happily with a—a proprietary
look, Andy decided.

"Hello! This is a surprise. Was the first week of school
so bad you had to have a weekend antidote this soon?"

"I haven't started yet. I've come—but I'd better let Dad
do the talking." Jay was fit to burst with excitement but
he repressed it as he turned to his father. So did everyone
else.

"I hadn't intended to spring it quite so fast. Thought I'd
wait until Mrs. Bard had one of her own good meals to
fortify her, but I can see if I don't, Jay will." The older
man paused momentarily to organize his words. "My business is taking me east for the winter but I don't want to
go unless Ella comes along. The two youngsters who aren't
in school can go with us, of course."

Andy flicked a lightning look at her mother as the same
thought struck.

"—But the other three don't want to go. Chuck and

Eleanor want to board at the school where they're day pupils now and that's all right with me if it is with them. But Jay—" Mr. Whitcomb's supplicating look skyward revealed to Andy what a tempest the Whitcombs had been in. "He won't consider anything but living at the Bar D and going to Valley High where Andy goes. Mrs. Bard, to save my sanity would you please consider boarding and looking after him for us?"

"I won't be a bit of trouble, Mrs. Bard." Jay's eagerness burned in every word he said. "I'll help around the ranch and study hard. I'm healthy too—you won't have to worry about my ever getting sick—"

Jay paused for breath, but still reading uncertainty in Mrs. Bard's expression he rushed on. "You'll be the boss, of course. I'll behave myself, but just so's you'll feel better about it I'll make a bargain with you. Take me on trial and if it doesn't work out you can send me back to the military school that Dad suggested. How's that?"

"Seems fair enough. All right, you can have the room next to Jump. When will you bring your things?"

"Right now. We brought everything in the back of the car." Jay yanked open the trunk and waved at bags, boxes, bundles, even a small trunk.

"We weren't actually that sure of your answer, Mrs. Bard," Jay's mother explained, "but he insisted it wouldn't hurt any to be ready. It does save us a second trip from Los Angeles, however, and we're really pressed for time."

"I'll bet old Sam just now shuddered like when you say someone's walking over your grave," Andy giggled.

"But, Andy! He doesn't need to. Dad says he'll buy me

a horse of my own. Of course, it won't be as good as Blue but if Luis can find one I can handle Sam can sleep in peace."

"Wonderful, Jay. Hey, you haven't heard. I'm making Blue a cutting horse and he's slightly sensational."

"I'd have heard if you'd written to me," he said reproachfully. "What is a cutting horse, one that cuts up? I thought Blue's days of that were over."

"No, no, a cutting horse is one that cuts cattle out of a herd—I'll tell you more about it later. As for a letter, I was waiting for you to write and tell me where Blue's papers are. Want to go down and see him?"

"Not now, Andy. Supper is on the table and I'm sure everyone's hungry. You and Jay will have all winter to ogle that wonder horse of yours."

Saturday morning Jay and his father drove over to see the high school principal at his home to handle the business details of enrollment. During their absence Andy, foreseeing a busy day ahead, gave Blue his workout. She found herself analyzing every move in order to explain it later to Jay, and this made it more vivid for herself.

Luis meanwhile had done some telephoning so the instant lunch was finished Andy, Jay, Luis and Mr. Whitcomb drove off in the yellow car in search of a satisfactory horse. Jay's excitement was at flood-tide at the start but one prospect after another was rejected, the animals being either unsound, too spirited or just plain plugs.

"Buying a horse isn't like buying a car, is it?" he said dolefully. "You can't just go down to the showroom and pick out one you want."

"No—or it's more like buying a car during war time. You have to find out what's available, then look it over carefully to see what shape it's in," Luis amended. "Cheer up though. We're going to Jim Blaine's place next. He generally has two or three to sell. Turn left at the next corner, Mr. Whitcomb."

Andy and Jay left the palaver to the grown ups and headed for the Blaine corrals when the car halted. There were several horses there, and they had to wait for their elders to know which ones were on the market.

"Got four for sale and I'll sell you any or all of 'em," Mr. Blaine drawled.

The first two he pointed out were indifferent nags, the third a nice-colored palomino, the fourth a rough-coated black. The latter two were saddled and Luis tried each one out before Jay stepped up.

"Which one do you like?" his father queried.

"I like 'em both," Jay replied, too thrilled with the proceedings to be very critical. "How about you, Luis?"

"If I were buying one, I'd take the black." Once sought, the foreman's decision was quick and positive.

"You would!" Jay's expression altered little but Andy could tell he favored the flashier palomino.

"Yes, he doesn't look so good now but he's young and will shape up fast. Then too, he has a better rein on him. The palomino is hard-mouthed and basically not as good conformation, but suit yourself, either one is a good buy."

"The palomino costs more," Jay protested as if that proved his excellence.

"Sure, you're paying for his color—like fancy wrappings

on a package. But it's the whole horse you ride. You'd g
a lot more pleasure out of the black."

Everyone was silent while Jay wrestled with the prob
lem. Mr. Whitcomb fidgeted slightly, wanting to get o
with the business of getting his son settled so he could g
back to his own affairs. Jay knew he must choose.

"I'll take the—" he began resolutely, only to pause an
gulp—"the black."

"Good for you, Jay. That's the one I liked." Andy wa
sure her friend had changed horses in mid-sentence. Sh
was equally sure it was a milestone in his life, that he wa
learning to accept another's judgment. "After all, you ca
improve a coat with some currying and grain but it's prett
hard to do anything about a horse that's heavy on the bit.

Mr. Whitcomb paid for the horse and they left, to retur
as soon as possible with the pick-up and horse trailer whic
Luis with his horse trading instinct had left at home. Jay
joy was complete when his new horse was at last turne
into the stall next to Blue.

"Mind you, you're not to take the horse to bed wit
you," Mrs. Bard laughed when Jay and Andy were finall
dragged in to supper.

"Nor you're not to go to bed with the horse," his mothe
completed.

"Just think, Jay," Andy chortled, "our horses will b
'Black and Blue' all the time."

·14·

Full Scale Hide-and-Seek

"Thought of a name for him yet?"

It was early Sunday morning and Andy and Jay were already out with the horses giving the black a vigorous grooming. The other Whitcombs had left for Los Angeles right after breakfast and the new horse owner had wasted little time between saying good-bye to them and hello to his black.

"Last night I thought of a dozen different names. Guess I'll settle on Black Magic though. During the past few days everything has worked like black magic and presto! here I am."

"That's slick, Jay. You'll even have a theme song, 'That old Black Magic's got me in *his* spell—"

" 'That old Black Magic that I love so well,' " Jay improvised as he joined in, a little farther off key than Andy was.

"Great duet we make. The next number should be Two Black Crows. Black Magic certainly has a fine head on him, practically a straight line from foretop to nose, a delicate muzzle and wonderful, wise eyes set well apart."

"You know, I think he looks better already." Jay stepped back to admire his horse again.

"Of course he does," Andy agreed wholeheartedly while understanding that much of the improvement could be attributed to pride of ownership. "He'll get better too right along."

"OK, let's get going ourselves. I'm perishing for a real ride on him."

Jay had learned to saddle and bridle a horse during the summer and the morning was still fresh when they were ready to mount. Bridle reins in hand, Andy walked over to open the gate into the first corral.

"That's to be ready for Blue's cutting lesson when we come back," she explained, at Jay's curious look. "The one thing that *I* can't cut is Blue's cutting. All aboard!"

Andy watched Black Magic so closely she felt as if she were riding two horses, for she was coaching Jay. Only the rudiments of riding had been touched on that summer, on the premise that a dude is always a dude, but now that he owned a horse of his own he was determined to do it right.

"Always treat a horse's mouth with tenderness and respect. Don't haul in on the reins like an emergency brake—unless it's a real emergency. And never, never, *never* jerk a horse's mouth for punishment, and don't use the reins to hang on with. If you lose your balance, grab the horn or the mane but don't jab his mouth with the bit. When you're just riding along and everything's rosy, ease up on the reins and go along with 'em loose—that's the mark of a good horse—and rider."

"Yes, miss. When can we gallop?"

"Hardly ever. A gallop is a dead run, but we can lope any time you want. Ready?"

The two horses swung off like twin rockers, Andy reveling in the black's responsiveness as though he were her own. The pace grew faster and faster.

"Don't lean forward. He thinks you want him to run. Just sit up straight easy-like. Check him on the bit a little, then let up, sort of like playing a trout on a line. That's it. Get the feel of that rocking-chair rhythm and ride it."

Jay and his horse were fast friends after that first ride. The blue stallion and black gelding liked each other too, so Andy was as happy as a mother hen with her brood. On the way home Jay and Black Magic pulled off to one

side while Andy and Blue rehearsed their footwork circ
to be ready for the steers. Jay and Black helped drive the
into the corral.

"He's worked cattle before and really knows his bu
ness," Andy remarked.

The girl chose Spatter out of turn to show Blue at l
best and the roan seemed to get the idea. He crouched a
wheeled and chivvied the animal back and forth with
the zest of a cat with a mouse. Once when the steer bro
away, Andy sensed that Blue purposely let it go for t
fun of bringing it back.

"How d'ya like that?" she exclaimed on dismountir
"It looks like I've got me a horse that's a grandstar
player."

Andy brushed a lock of hair off her damp forehead wi
one hand and tousled Blue's foretop with the other.

"What makes you think so?" Jay rode into the corr
seeing Andy had finished.

"He's never done so well—he always has zip and da
but today he was a real show-off and I declare I think i
because you were watching. Well, that's all to the goo
Blue. Before we're through I hope there'll be hundre
times one to cheer you on."

Andy begrudged every tick of Sunday's clock for
nibbled away at her play time, inexorably drawing Mo
day morning nearer until it was upon her. The four
them were waiting at the gate for their school buses.

"Yes, ma'am, this certainly is an occasion," Jay observe
airily.

Andy bit. "Why, 'cause you're starting a new school today?"

"No. Now at last I've seen you in a skirt. You should do it more often. It's very becoming."

"Don't worry," Andy snapped dourly, "you'll see me in a skirt five days a week for nine months now."

Her pink cheeks were not entirely due to the morning coolness and, too late, she wished that she had worn her new gabardine dress rather than her favorite old skirt and sweater. No, that wouldn't have been a good idea either.

She hoped that Jay could slip easily into the student body but she wondered nervously how his city ways and brash manner would go in a country school. The girls, she knew, would fall all over each other to welcome him, but if Jay's winter was to be a pleasant one he must have masculine approval too.

"Do you play football? Are you going out for the team?" she asked hopefully.

"I like basketball and baseball better but, of course," Jay coughed deprecatingly, "my marks have never been high enough to give athletics a try."

"That's foolish." Andy was basically too thrifty to waste anything, even schooling.

"Yes, I guess it is," he agreed disarmingly. "I've resolved to work like the dickens this fall. But you'll have to help me."

"A lot of help I'll be when you're a year ahead."

"Maybe all it'll take is a quirt in your right hand."

Groaning brakes on the opposite grade alerted them for the bus. With a lifetime's practice Andy synchronized her step up with the halting of the bus and the opening door.

"Hey, everybody, this is Jay Whitcomb. He's going to live at the Bar D this year and go to school at Valley High. Now it's up to all of you to tell him your own names."

Introductions progressed while the bus bowled along the highway. Andy sat back in her seat. There was nothing more she could do; from here on Jay was on his own. By the time school ended for the day, Andy concluded that Jay had inherited much of his father's salesmanship and charm, for not once had she seen him by himself.

On the home-bound bus he seemed to fit in naturally, as though he had been doing it all his life, but by now Andy's attention centered on her date with Blue. Well in advance of the Bar D stop she had her books and jacket and purse organized for a quick get-away. Blue was no greater magnet for her, however, than Black Magic was for Jay. They jumped off the bus and scurried up the long driveway like a couple of squirrels.

"Race you to the stable," he challenged on reaching the house.

"No fair! You don't have to change clothes like I do— Even so you'll have to hustle some."

Jay won on a technicality as Mrs. Bard waylaid Andy to ask about Jay's first day. On arriving at the stable Andy found that Blue had been brushed down and Jay was giving Black a dutch rub. They saddled quickly and rode away.

The horses' quick steps drummed on the sod like muffled tom-toms. Andy wondered idly whether someone versed in Indian drum talk could catch their meaning. So clearly defined a rhythm must be saying something—perhaps telling the whereabouts of the lost papers. She half-closed her eyes to pinpoint her whole attention on the sound but she could make no more of it than a double four-beat.

" 'S funny about Blue's papers," Jay remarked. Andy's eyes widened with surprise. She was startled to find that her telepathy set had been sending rather than receiving. "They've got to be on the ranch somewhere since you have all of Pop's belongings there."

A chill ran down Andy's spine so she could only squeak a reply. "Not quite everything. The coroner took his car and trailer away to be sold before I had a chance to check them thoroughly. Of course, the glove compartment was cleaned out."

"What about under the seats?"

Andy shook her head miserably, astonished at herself for not having thought of such a possibility.

"But Pop had taken everything into his cabin. He'd never leave anything so important in the car," she argued, trying to convince herself as much as Jay.

"Yeah, you're right—but it is a possibility. Let's go to Santa Barbara with Luis Saturday and see if we can find the car."

"All right, but we'll have to phone Mr. Hedges first. The courthouse is closed Saturday mornings."

During the intervening days as Andy hurried to school, to Blue, to her homework, her thoughts raced ahead toward Saturday. By telephone she had learned that the car had been sold to a used car dealer who in turn had sold it to a young fellow with no telephone. The trailer was still in the county yard awaiting a buyer.

Andy's hopes floated like dandelion fluff, first up, then down, but by Saturday morning they had steadied at a high level. She and Jay had convinced themselves the papers were as good as in her hands. Their first stop was at the county yard to check the trailer, but that took only a few minutes.

There was no tack compartment and the manger was empty. The sides and flooring were obviously single-plank construction, leaving no possible crannies for anything larger than a gum wrapper, but the three of them, Luis, Andy and Jay, probed and rapped and pounded until they were satisfied.

"I didn't think they'd be there anyway," Andy admitted gaily. "Now, Luis, to 1206 San Pascual Street."

Luis turned the station wagon toward Santa Barbara's west side.

"Do you want the car to break into a gallop?" Jay chided. "You're leaning forward far enough for a stretch drive."

"Maybe that's what this is." Andy laughed happily, but sat back for a moment nevertheless, although within two blocks she resumed her expectant pose. "There's a car in front of the house—but it isn't the old Ford." A little of her exuberance drained away with this admission.

Luis stopped behind the other car, a would-be hot rod. Andy took the front steps two at a time and rang the bell. No answer. She pushed the button again and while she could hear no bell she felt sure it worked because a dog in the backyard barked. She turned away irresolutely, standing on the top step. Should she leave a note? Or go around to the back door? The doorknob rattled and Andy whirled to see a sleepy-eyed young fellow behind the screen.

"Oh, I'm sorry to have disturbed you," she apologized but plunged on feverishly. "I'm hoping you can help me. Did you buy a '38 Ford from Honest Tom's used car lot on lower State Street a while ago?"

Too thick with sleep for speech, the other gestured wordlessly at the car out in front.

"No-o-o!"

Andy's distress was so real he collected himself enough to talk. "I just kept the chassis and junked the body."

"You did! Where is it? You see"—she felt he was entitled to some explanation after being roused from his sleep—"we've lost something and we think, at least we *hope*, it might be in the car. Did you find anything under the seats or—or anyplace?"

"Nary a thing—but you can see for yourself if you want. I hauled it to the city dump and it's probably still there. You'd recognize it, wouldn't you?"

"I—I think so, but I'm not sure. It wasn't mine and it'll look kind of different."

The house was near enough the street for Luis and Jay to hear the conversation. The latter poked his head out the window.

"Come along and show us where it is and we'll set you up to a ham'n egg breakfast."

"Oh, please do," Andy seconded.

"OK, I'll be out in a mo'."

Introductions were made after he climbed into the ca
Andy was thankful young Hoffman had come along whe
they turned into the dump. Such a jumble of old car
plumbing, lumber and scrap she had never seen. Luis looke
to Hoffman for directions.

"Straight ahead a little ways and then we'll have to g
out."

All four scrambled out where Hoffman indicated. H
looked around to get his bearings but a puzzled expressio
settled on his face, accelerating Andy's heartbeat. Suddenl
he pointed to the bottom of a ravine.

"There! That's it clear down there. Guess some kic
gave it a push to watch it roll down hill—and it sure did.

Luis thoughtfully armed himself with an ax but th
others rushed headlong down to the battered derelict. Th
torn seats had been rattled around on the downhill trip an
it was plain to see nothing remained in the compartmen
beneath. Andy rechecked the glove box and trunk whil
Jay was ripping the cushions apart with a jackknife. Lu
knocked the upholstering loose from the front and rea
seat backs but to no avail.

"The papers just aren't here." Andy's admission wa
almost a dirge.

"Papers! What papers?" their guide asked quickly.

"My Quarter Horse's registration papers." Andy tele
scoped the whole story in five words.

"Well, hey, what about inside the doors? Or up unde
the dash?"

A possible mystery caught Hoffman's attention. He kicked in the paneling on one door and ripped off the fabric covering while the others fell to with equal vigor, each to a door. No long envelope such as Andy saw in her dreams fell out, however. Hoffman tore the cardboard from under the cowl and, lighting a match, he peered into the recess behind the dash. Jay meanwhile had had another brainstorm. Slashing the ceiling fabric he janked it off the cross pieces with the same result. Nothing.

All four of them, including Hoffman, stood around the demolished car like chief mourners. Andy poked dispiritedly at the piles of dirty white stuffing.

"Anybody got any other bright ideas?" Her question was really no question at all. "Well, I guess that's one more place the papers aren't."

Each new lead that fizzled to a dud left her more disheartened than before. Today for the first time she admitted to herself, but to no one else, that perhaps she never would find the papers. Or, a new angle struck her, maybe Blue did not have papers. Many older people had done stranger things than convince themselves their pets were registered. But that was no reason for Pop's not insuring her uncontested ownership of Blue. That had been dearer to his heart than anything else toward the last.

Andy had little appetite for a second breakfast or any of the city attractions but her spirits rose slightly when the station wagon was headed home. The nearer they got to the Bar D the better she felt. Luis and Jay noted her improvement.

"Looks like you're just a country girl at heart," the latter said.

"No, I don't think it's that. It's more like being told when you're getting 'hot' or 'cold.' I'm playing full-scale hide-and-seek for those papers, and somehow I feel they're close to home."

·15·

Cowboy from Los Angeles

It was still early afternoon when they returned to the Bar D. Jay wanted to ride to a nearby hilltop where he thought there was a hawk's nest, but Andy let him go off alone as she was impatient to get on with Blue Smoke's training.

After a good long walk down creek they cut their warm-up circles, following which the steers were herded in from pasture. Instead of driving three on into the second corral as she had been doing, Andy hesitated. It would be wrong to hurry the horse. So long as they worked just one animal in the corral at a time it could never really get away from Blue, but with all four there each steer would try harder to rejoin the others.

"We've been working them one at a time for weeks and weeks, Blue. Let's try just once anyway. We'll pick on Baldy, he's the slowest of the lot and oughn't to push you very much."

The stallion proved immediately that he was ready for this promotion by controlling the steer masterfully from start to finish. Too smart to push her luck too far, thereafter Andy was content to practice with just one steer in the corral at a time.

"That was big-time stuff, Bluesy, if I ever saw it," she

praised him while she was putting him away. "I wish Jay had seen it."

At supper she waited for just the right opening to begin bragging about Blue's newest feat. Before she had such a chance Mrs. Bard dealt her the day's second blow.

"Don't forget to set your clocks back an hour tonight. Daylight Saving Time ends at one in the morning."

"Daylight Saving ends! Oh, this is terrible. Why, it'll be almost dark when we get home from school. It will be later on," Andy wailed. "How'll I ever find enough daylight hours to keep Blue going?"

"It ends the last Sunday every September," her mother said mildly. "You ought to remember that much."

This sent Andy's spirits down for the count. She couldn't expect Blue to cut cattle in the dark. The sun shone the same number of hours, of course, that hour of daylight just came in the morning now.

Sunday, the first day back on Standard Time, Andy decided to find out how the hour worked at the beginning rather than the end of the day. She set her alarm to go off at dawn and, slipping into her jeans, she hurried out to the stable to saddle Blue.

At the conclusion of his "finger exercises" the cattle were driven in from pasture and cutting practice proceeded as usual. After putting Blue away, without any short cuts, Andy raced to the house and looked at the clock.

"Check! I can work him mornings for a while until the days get too short. Sure can't dawdle any though."

Thenceforth "dawdle" was a word that Andy met only in books. Her days moved on split-second timing from her early appointment with Blue through school, her Bar D duties, homework and bed in time to arise for her solitary dawn patrol again. After one try Jay bowed out of the early morning exercises.

So October went and part of November. Andy found that as the days shortened mornings were grayer and grayer which meant that soon her early morning rides would have to end, for dark was dark whether before sunrise or after sundown. One cold, gusty evening that warned of winter's imminence everyone gathered in the living room where a grate fire warmed their hearts as well as their bodies. Luis, looking up from the bridle he was mending, spoke to Andy.

"Is that cutting horse of yours ready to meet cattle, plural, yet?"

"Sure. Why, when and how many?"

"Armistice Day is Sunday next so I expect you'll get a Monday holiday, and I figured that long weekend would be a good time to reclassify the herd. How about you, Jay? Feel up to some real cowboying?"

"Just say the word and it'll all be done with 'Magic.'"

"I'll help, Luis. Count me in." Jump volunteered eagerly.

"I am. You and Sam will get all the work you can handle before you're through."

Every day that week Blue practiced with the four steers in the corral with him although Andy was extra careful. She worked Baldy two days in a row, then Freckles and Spatter. The horse handled them skillfully. If it seemed one might get out of hand, Blue was pulled up to guard against feeling it had slipped past his defenses.

Friday morning Andy surveyed her little herd critically. The part-Brahma had had no work at all and looked fat and sassy.

"How about it, Blue? Shall we take him on for sort of a final examination? He'll likely give you a run for your money."

He did, but Blue was not to be shaken. After a few light-ning turns Andy felt the horse had passed his finals with flying colors. She quit while they were ahead.

"That'll hold us 'til tomorrow, boy, when we'll really find out if you've got what it takes."

Luis and his riders set out promptly the next morning to gather the cattle from all parts of the Bar D. The grass was dried up and tasteless so until the rains came the cattle would require supplementary feeding which would be easier at headquarters.

"Black has certainly improved like magic. He's quite a horse already."

Andy had been surveying Jay's mount critically as the four rode out into the lower pasture.

"He always was one. He has been somebody's top horse or I miss my guess," Luis surmised. "Looks like he expects it to be a cold, wet winter from the overcoat he's wearing."

"It's smooth though and shines like a blackbird's wing. I'll bet he'll know what to do with an ornery critter all right, all right."

Jay took no part in the conversation but he lapped it up, praise of his horse being even better than praise of himself. He stroked the coal-black neck on the pretext of brushing off a fly.

Luis led them to the line fence where they fanned out to start homeward. One bunch of cattle after another was added to the main drive, the noise and dust making it look like the old Chisholm Trail. Frequently Jay or Jump or both were left to keep the herd moving while Luis and Andy scoured the side canyons and brush-covered hillsides for singles.

The first time Jay was left alone to keep the cattle moving, he was filled with a panic he'd never have admitted, but Black was not dismayed. With teeth and thrusting shoulder he asserted his domination over the cattle until it was a determined loiterer that risked his displeasure. His rider gained confidence rapidly on learning that cattle cling together instinctively as well as drawing others to them. Jay was ready when Luis sent him out for a straggler. He and Black circled back to come up behind it. Slapping his thigh as he had seen the others do to start it moving, he brought it into the herd like a proud retriever.

"Good stuff! We'll make a cowboy of you yet," Luis applauded.

"Yeah, the cowboy from Los Angeles—that's me."

The herd was held in the small pasture overnight and Sunday, while they cleared the upper pasture. Andy's thoughts reverted to Pop and his last ride there, setting her mind to revolving in its same old squirrel cage.

"That's where we found Pop's billfold," she told Jay, nodding her head to the left.

"What's your next step in searching for the papers? I've been wondering but hated to bring it up after that last disappointment."

"Can't think of a thing. I have been thinking though that maybe this is a lot of fuss and fury over nothing. I've got the horse and I guess they mean to let me keep him, so why worry?"

"That's just playing ostrich, Andrea Bard, and you know it. That letter proves Pop had a son, his legal heir. Perhaps he won't ever show up, but if he ever hears that Pop left a valuable horse you aren't going to have time to find the papers or whatever Pop left giving you title to Blue. Right?"

"All right, smarty, go into a trance and come up with a hot tip."

Andy called her challenge across a widening distance as

she veered to the right for the homeward drive which proceeded smoothly. This upper pasture held cows and calves that ambled peaceably before the riders, little knowing what harrowing experiences lay ahead.

This bunch was pushed into the big corral. One by one the mothers were cut off and turned back into pasture until their next trip with new offspring. Not all cows, however, had calves. Some of these were returned to pasture while others at a signal from Luis, were turned into a different corral to be sold.

The two gatherings had been comparatively easy but this separating tested the skill of both horses and riders. Some cows were determined not to have their young ones taken away. Luis and his bay handled these. Andy, Jay and Jump took turns with the others.

Blue proved himself every inch a cutting horse. Black, too, though by no means as finished as Blue, showed that he knew how to handle the critters, more than once giving his "cowboy from Los Angeles" reason to hang on. The last cut was made as the sun dipped behind a tree-fringed hill. Then Luis paid off his help with a compliment.

"There! That'd be a good day's work on any ranch, thanks to my fine help. Sounds as if we're in for a noisy night, eh?"

It did indeed, with the anxious mothers mooing for their young that were bawling lustily for their supper of warm milk. Outside in the lower holding pasture the other cattle lowed restlessly, knowing these were uneasy times.

"After something to eat, I could sleep through an earthquake-cyclone-thunderstorm," Jay sighed, "but isn't it great? I wouldn't have missed it for a dozen prep schools. 'That old Black Magic's got me in his spell,' " he sang happily, riding toward the stables.

The cattle truck was due late Monday afternoon, so Luis and his hands were up and out while it was still cool enough to need a jacket. A good night's rest and hearty food, whether it was oats and hay or steak and potatoes, had restored everyone to peak efficiency. The work was much the same as on the afternoon before, cutting out the stock to be sold, the heifers to go into a different bunch, shoving a few that needed doctoring into a chute.

Andy was so encouraged by Blue's performance the preceding day she grew more ambitious and deliberately chose animals that might tax her horse's powers. She kept her reining to a minimum. When the reins flapped loose on a turn, proving that Blue did it without a cue, she was fit to burst with pride.

"You great, big, wonderful horse, you," she crowed during a short recess. "Maybe I should have been bringing you on faster than I did."

"By Jupiter, I can see how cutting can get to be a malady. Why didn't Black and I start earlier?"

"For one thing you needed to get the feel of your horse first. Cutting riding is no cinch but it's a pity that you've caught the fever just as our daylight hours are numbered—except for weekends—and that's not enough."

"You think Black really shows promise?"

"Sure enough! Oh, he'll probably not hit the big-time but he'd provide you with a lot of fun."

"Do you expect Blue to get into the upper brackets of cutting horses?"

"I certainly do. I hope he'll make the top ten next year, but I guess that's kind of optimistic."

"Top ten?"

"Yeah, the cutting horse people keep a monthly record of horses' winnings; they figure each dollar won is one point. The national champion is the horse with the highest number of points—or dollars. Competition ends with the show at the San Francisco Cow Palace which just closed, so by this time next fall I hope a lot more people will know about the Bar D, Home of Blue Smoke, than do at present."

Sorting operations resumed then and there was no more time for talk until the last animal had joined the proper bunch. They finished not a minute too soon, for before the dust had settled the livestock truck pulled into the yard and backed up to the loading chute. Luis and the driver pushed the cattle in rapidly. When the truck pulled away, Jay thought the work was finished and started to unsaddle.

"Wait a minute; we aren't through yet," Luis remonstrated.

"We aren't? What comes now?"

"We have to pick out some new stock for Andy and Blue to work and then—"

"Luis, I won't be able to work Blue many more mornings—anyone in her right mind wouldn't try to at all—and I've been wondering whether it's worth it to keep any cattle in just for weekends."

"That gives me an opening," Jay interrupted, "to bring up an idea I just had. Mrs. Bard, would you mind if we strung up some floodlights over one corral? That way Andy and I could work our horses any time."

"I wouldn't mind a bit, Jay, but this tells me," Mrs. Bard flipped the receipt she had just been handed for the market cattle, "that I can't spare the money to buy lights."

"Oh, I didn't mean that. I'd like to pay for them if you'll let me, and I think I can get some of the guys from school to help me install them if you'll just furnish the electricity. How about that?"

"I'd be a piker indeed not to agree to that proposition." Mrs. Bard smiled. "Sounds as if the cutting craze is contagious."

"Oh, Jay! That's really de luxe. Now we can work all winter long. Will you have to write your father for the money?"

"No, they give me an allowance every month but I don't seem to spend it here the way I do in Los Angeles. Besides, I'd rather have floodlights than gimcracks any day—or should I say night?"

·16·

First Step

Andy was to remember that winter for its lights: brilliant floodlights over the corral, colored Christmas tree lights, soft lights at school parties, study lamps, the glowing fireplace when rain and wind lashed the house viciously, and one morning bright, warm sunlight that signaled the arrival of California's spring.

Andy resumed the dawn patrol, with Jay an eager second this time. Blue had progressed so rapidly he now worked with all the cattle in the corral and he needed a hazer—a part Jay could fill easily. When cattle were separated from the herd and bolted for the unoccupied end of the arena, Jay's job as hazer was to turn them back toward Andy, the cutter. Caught between the two horsemen, the beef was likely to exhibit some close, fast action that showed the cutting horse off to better advantage than if he had merely chased the steer around the farther limits of the arena.

The Santa Ynez Valley Horse Show, a two-day affair, was slated for late March at a neighboring, very prosperous guest ranch. Andy entered Blue in the cutting horse class which not only strained her financial resources but looked like reckless extravagance inasmuch as the show was attracting some of the Coast's top-flight horses.

Blue looked as fit as grooming and regular exercise could make him. As an added precaution Andy persuaded her mother and Luis to let her have a larger herd to practice on the last few days, thinking that the horse might be confused to find fifteen or twenty head milling around in the show arena. It made no difference to Blue, however. If anything it showed him to better advantage.

"There, fellow. That winds us up. I'm counting on you to put on a good show for us."

Blue was to have a day's rest to build up extra ginger for the show, so in this final practice Andy had been as critical as she knew how, yet he satisfied her at every turn. Friday, however, a bit of news she picked up at school sent her soaring hopes plummeting downward. She practically fell off the bus in her haste to tell the family.

"I'm going to scratch Blue tomorrow. I'm not going to ride him in that class at all—not even in the first go-round tomorrow."

"Heavenly days! What's got into you now? This morning you could hardly wait for the hours to pass."

"Tom Hansen's father is handling show entries and Tom told me this morning there isn't a single other local horse in the cutting class—they're all well-known horses and riders, some from as far away as northern California. Blue and I will look like ninnies."

"You're going to have to face 'em sometime, Andy, or Blue'll never be tops."

"Now's as good a time as any to show 'em how it's done."

"There's an old proverb that says something to the effect

that you can't make a trip around the world without taking the first step."

Jay, Luis and Mrs. Bard each tried to buoy her up but it was Jump who really scored.

"Ah-h, you're just scairt. You'll feel all right once you get going."

"You probably are a little nervous, dear. Better get to bed early and tomorrow things will look brighter."

Mrs. Bard's mother instinct was partially correct. Andy did feel better the next morning while she was occupied getting Blue and her tack cleaned and ready to trailer to the show. She managed to hold on to some composure on the ride over, but the cutting class was the very last thing on the program. As hunters, jumpers, stock horses, trail horses had their turns Andy's fingernails took more and more punishment.

She saddled Blue with meticulous care and rode well away from the arena to warm him up. Just as though they were at home getting ready to work the Bar D cattle, Andy put him into a tight circle to the left, then to the right. Off alone with her horse she regained her equanimity.

"You may not win anything, old boy, 'cause we're both pretty green, but we'll be in there trying every minute."

Blue knew enough about crowds to sense that he was again before the public and he strutted vaingloriously as Andy guided him around behind the scenes while waiting for their class to be called. When the preceding class was in the ring all cutting contestants were called together to draw lots for their order of appearance. There were eight in all and Andy found that she was the only girl as well as the youngest rider.

"Ladies first," the official said as he passed an upturned sombrero to her to pull out a number.

Andy took a deep breath, exhaling in a silent prayer, as her fingers found a wadded paper and handed it to the man.

"Ladies first, for sure! You drew first place."

"Too bad." "Tough luck." "It might work out all right." The other riders murmured sympathetically or hopefully according to their own preferences for position. Andy was now scared clear through. Generally this spot was a handicap since at first the cattle were restless and uneasy from being pushed around whereas later contestants could enter the herd with a minimum of disturbance. Even discounting this consideration Andy had hoped for a short respite between entering the arena and taking her turn to permit her to see how her opponents and their high-ranking horses went about their task.

The jumpers finished their stint in the ring and departed. Down at the far end cowboys were driving a milling mob of whitefaced Herefords into the ring while the announcer reviewed the rules for the benefit of those unfamiliar with cutting classes.

"Each horse has two minutes to work—thirty-second warning—may work as many cattle as desired—penalties for reining, spurring or otherwise cuing the horse—each rider works with a hazer to turn the animals back—"

"Gotta pick ourselves a hazer, Blue. Which one do you like?"

Andy surveyed the others critically. Which one to ask?

To approach one of the leaders would seem pretty pre-
sumptuous, she felt, but there was another, a lean young
man who rode a good-looking sorrel.

"Would you haze for me?" She tried desperately to keep

her tone light, her smile just the right combination of off-
hand friendliness, but her voice quavered on the last words.

"I sure enough would. Any special instructions?"

"Nope. You probably know what's wanted better than
I do. Oh, oh! Here we go."

The loudspeaker called for Andy Bard and Blue Smoke
of the Bar D and she started him toward the herd. He was

not affected one little bit by stage fright and sidled into the packed cattle almost tenderly while Andy's head whirled. Which one should it be? Her choice might make or break Blue's chances for a good show.

Right on the edge of the herd one white face liberally dotted with red beckoned to her like an old friend and Andy gratefully chose this one that reminded her of Spatter. She reined Blue behind it to indicate her choice and he peeled it off as easily as a sheet of paper. The steer ambled along the fence with mock docility until he saw his chance. Turning at right angles he scatted straight across the ring. When Blue headed him off on the other side Spatter II whipped about and ran the other way.

Andy wasn't looking for a race, she wanted a steer that dodged and doubled. Her right hand went up to signify that she was dropping that one and rode back for a second. It was almost impossible to ride into the nervous herd without exciting them. One stubborn one refused to be afraid so Blue nipped his tail to move him.

"OK, boy, we'll take that red one."

Blue shouldered him out, the other cattle happily giving way although wily Red tried to hide behind every steer near him. Just as they cleared the pack Andy heard the thirty-second warning and hoped that Red would give them some real action. He did. His footwork was speed plus as he turned and twisted to shake his tormentor, but Blue was faster on his feet and he seemed to read Red's mind as well. Head to head they bobbed and jived like a couple of hepcats on a crowded floor.

So split-second was their action, Andy couldn't have

thought fast enough to cue Blue had she wanted to and the reins flapped loose. It was all she could do to stay in the saddle, riding the lunges forward, sideways, a quick back step. Her mind closed out everything else so completely it was seconds after time was called before she understood and pulled up.

"Boy, Blue! I wish we'd gotten that one first. The other was a dud and never gave you a chance to strut your stuff."

"Say, your horse is just a little bit of all right," her hazer exclaimed. "Who trained him?"

"I did," she said matter-of-factly, "or, more like it, I gave him a chance to develop his talents."

Andy's hopes soared, not for that show particularly but for Blue's future. Some of the others had more finish, the result of longer experience she surmised, but with practice Blue would be able to hold his own.

From reading the rules book she knew that horses were scored between sixty and eighty points with seventy an average. Keeping this in mind she tried scoring the seven contestants only to become all bogged down in figures. Nevertheless when the last critter had been cut in that day's Go Round, Andy believed that Blue was somewhere in the middle, better than several, not as good as some. If he showed as well or better in the next day's Go Round his combined score for the two days should put him somewhere in the money.

"Luis," she asked on the way home, "is there any way to tell from a steer's looks how he will act? If that first one today had been as salty as the second, we'd have looked pretty good."

"No more than you can tell by looking at a frog how far it can jump. Maybe once in a while there'll be some clue that'll help you but mostly it's just one of those things you have to leave to your intuition."

Although Andy felt like a veteran after her first plunge she was able to keep only half her attention on Sunday's classes. She enjoyed the jumping and stock horse events in a remote sort of way but left happily to get Blue ready well in advance of the cutting class. Lady Luck was kinder to her in the drawing, for she and Blue were assigned third place.

"That's just perfect, Blue. Gives the cattle time enough to settle down, but they haven't yet been chivvied all over the lot."

A fresh bunch was brought in and the first contestant rode out for his two minutes, followed by the second. At a nod from the judge Andy settled herself into her saddle and rode Blue across the starting line where timing commenced.

Two minutes later when she rode Blue back after the final whistle her inner elation boiled explosively high. If Blue's was not a winning performance, the others would have to go some to beat it, Andy exulted silently although her face was impassive.

"Wow, this cutting riding may look like a sedentary occupation but it's pretty rough stuff," she said ruefully to the lanky hazer to cover her real feelings. "Thanks a lot for helping me out."

"Glad to do it. I'm afraid to have you haze for me—your horse would make mine look like a stumblebum."

The five succeeding contestants had varying success.

Andy followed their every move fearfully. If only the previous day's highs did not do so well, they would all average out and Blue would be high horse. They were not all so obliging, however, but after the last whistle had been blown and the results had been added to the previous day's scores Andy was jubilant to find that Blue was fifth.

"That's good enough for me—to start with," she rejoiced to the Bar D folks who met her outside the gate. "It proves we're on the right track and—to be very practical about it— we got our entry money back with enough for a grubstake in the next cutting class. We've taken that first step, so where do we go from here?"

"I don't know about you," Mrs. Bard said wearily, "but I'll settle for just going home."

·17·

Chest X-ray

Hopes ran high at the Bar D after Blue's good showing the Valley show and Andy worked on him with wh souled concentration. Results of the show were written in some stock horse magazines, so she watched the m nervously, jumped when the telephone rang, lest some turn up to claim her horse. The weeks went by, howe with no contenders appearing.

Andy felt that opportunity was knocking right on saddlehorn when she learned that the Pacific Coast Quar Horse Association's annual show was to be held in Sa Barbara. She knew it would attract top horses from m; of the western states so being anywhere in the mo would skyrocket Blue's reputation overnight. She wr immediately for entry blanks.

Luis planted a seed of doubt in her mind before th had been time to hear from the Quarter Horse peop Their reply confirmed the awful truth. It was a show clo to everything but registered Quarter Horses, requiring hibitors to have either the papers or the registration numl

Andy was not easily discouraged, writing back by reti mail to give Blue's full name, that of his sire and dam well as Pop's complete name, with the request for horse's number. With equal promptness the association asked her to furnish a bill of sale or copy of her lease, if that was how she had possession of the horse, before he could be permitted to show.

Still not daunted Andy phoned Mr. Hedges at the court-house to ask for some official proof of her rights to the horse but that canny gentleman was loath to oblige. Any-thing sufficiently authoritative to satisfy the Quarter Horse Association would be equivalent to assigning legal owner-ship to the girl.

Andy's blood pressure boiled higher and higher during this exchange. Even a pleading letter, explaining the cir-cumstances in detail, failed to so much as modify their demands, but the ultimatum closed cordially with an in-vitation to join the association if she was not already a member.

"What's the use of joining if they don't recognize that I own a Quarter Horse?" she asked herself plaintively, jamming the letter back in its envelope as she and Jay walked up the driveway after school.

"Bad news, I gather."

"Not good. Looks like I'm licked. Here the show of shows is about to be held practically on my doorstep and I can't enter Blue. Oh, where could Pop have put those papers?" Andy's question was almost a wail. "He'd never have hidden them for keeps."

"He intended to tell you where they were, but perhaps no one else, so they aren't just lying around loose any-where. I've been saying all along you ought to find them before you wanted them in a hurry—and now you do."

"All right, wise guy! You talk as if I haven't been tr
ing."

Quick-tempered though Jay was himself, he never g
mad at the same time Andy did. "When we find 'em, w
think how silly we were not to have guessed long ago."

"*If* we find them. I'm just about whipped. I'm all out
ideas."

"Just for fun, start clear back at the beginning and t
me everything about you and Pop and Blue."

"Well, once upon a time—" Andy opened her narrati
facetiously.

There was a short intermission while she changed cloth
Then the story continued through part of their ride, en
ing with her leaving Pop on the porch when she took t
dudes riding.

"You say you've checked the chest? I suppose it's ji
because Pop gave it to you the same time he said Blue w
to be yours that makes me keep wondering about it."

"I suppose. Me too. I've checked it over and over a doz
times, but it's always just an empty little box."

"Bring it into the living room tonight and let's give
another going-over."

When Andy went to supper she took the chest with h
She and Jay went into a huddle over it as soon as th
finished eating, rapping and thumping in turn while t
other listened intently for the minutest difference in tor

"What you two need is an old-fashioned magician w
could read a newspaper through a layer of cloth." M
Bard chuckled.

"Yeah, or else hold it up to a bright light," Jump gu
fawed.

"Hey, that's an idea!" Jay cried. "Why haven't we thought of it before?"

"No bright lights, I guess." Andy thought he too was trying to be funny.

"No, seriously. Supposing you broke an arm, or something. What would the doctor do?"

"Have it x-rayed." Andy almost shouted the answer. "Why *haven't* we thought of it before? Happy day! Let's make an appointment for Saturday—that's the first day we can get into town. Muz, Luis is going then, isn't he?"

"Yes, luckily. I can tell he'd have to make a trip whether he needed to or not."

"Jiminy! If the x-ray helped us any—and we found the you-know-whats—I'll bet I could still get an entry in in time for that show. Two whole days yet 'til Saturday. Muz, I don't suppose you'd consider—?"

"No, I would not consider letting you miss school for any such wild goose chase."

"This is no wild goose chase, Mrs. Bard," Andy replied with mock stiffness. "This is the hottest idea yet. I've felt all along—"

"That the papers were in Pop's cabin—or his billfold—or the old car—or else surely in the chest." Her mother smiled. "It's a good enough idea, but not worth a day's schooling. Saturday's soon enough. It'll give you that much more time to hope."

Promptly at ten o'clock Saturday morning Andy and Jay entered the x-ray office to be greeted by a pleasant-faced woman wearing a white uniform.

"Which one of you is to have the chest x-ray?" she inquired.

"Neither of us—it's this chest."

Andy laughed and pointed to the chest which Ja
on the desk. Andy sketched their problem to explain
strange request, but the woman was not encouraging.

"I seriously doubt whether the x-ray would disclose
sort of thing. It might, if the printing happened to h
high percentage of lead in it, but it's such a gamble I'r
sure it's worth the expense."

"Oh, let's take a chance," Jay insisted. "How long
it be after taking the pictures before we'll know?"

"If I'm no busier than I am now, I can develop
right away. Bring the chest in here."

The two young folks watched through a window
the technician took several shots of the chest from all
Then they returned to the reception room to wait. /
riffled through magazine after magazine but none of
had anything as fascinating as her own mystery story.
instant her hopes would shoot up like a leaf in a b
only to hit a down draft and crash the moment after.

The inner door opened and they leaped to their feet
the technician's expression told them the bad news be
she spoke.

"I can't find a thing in the pictures. Come in and se
yourselves."

One after another the negatives were placed on a l
lighted rack. Andy and Jay squinted and stared una
ingly for not so much as a speck of dust appeared or
plates. The pair were too crestfallen for speech and
woman shared their disappointment.

"That is too bad. I must admit I had hoped somet

might show up but I didn't want to sound as if I was talking you in to it."

They thanked her and Jay insisted on paying for the x-rays.

"After all, it was my idea," he told Andy, "and if we'd found the papers I'd have taken all the credit for being so smart. I might as well take the whole burden."

Jay did not give up easily on the chest and that evening after supper he picked it up again from the table where Andy had left it. He fingered it speculatively.

"Let's take it apart, Andy. What d'ya say?"

"No! It'd be a crime to ruin an heirloom like that on such a wild chance."

"Suppose the papers *are* in it. You'll never get them otherwise."

"They can't be—any more than they were in all those other places. The little chest would look like the old car did, all its stuffing out and everything, and we wouldn't be any farther ahead. And even if they are there," Andy reasoned, "Pop didn't have to tear it to pieces to put them in, so there'd have to be an easier way."

"That's right. It is beautiful workmanship too. Just look at how its sides dovetail together at the corners, neater'n any jigsaw puzzle."

"And it isn't as if it was something that could be duplicated in a store—I'll bet you wouldn't find another chest like that now outside of a museum."

There was no post entry for Andy in the Quarter Horse Show but she and Jay and Luis attended both day's performances although it strained her good nature to the breaking point. She was not the inactive spectator type and her companions could scarcely keep track of proceedings for her disgruntled comments.

"Blue could do better'n that." "Look at that horse—doesn't know which way he's going." "They call that a Quarter Horse?" "What's that horse got that Blue hasn't got?"

To this Luis leaned over to answer softly, "Registration papers." Andy took the hint and subsided although she continued to glower at the fortunate ones in the ring. Watching the cutting class from the grandstand was refined torture but it had its advantages since she was able to observe every move of horse, rider and critter. This only served to make her feel worse, for not a horse there did any better than she knew Blue could have done.

Andy was deep in the doldrums for the last few weeks of school and the final dismissal cheered her but little. The Whitcombs had a family reunion at the Bar D the first week of vacation and Andy briefly rejoiced with Jay when his eloquence, coupled with good marks, convinced his father that he should be permitted to spend the summer there.

Together they rode in some small shows with moderate success. Andy and Blue took first place in a Santa Barbara show's cutting class for novice horses while Jay was the happiest person in California when Black Magic placed fourth in the same class.

"You're doing just fine with him," Andy exclaimed later. "Now if you'll work on your own riding it'll help him a lot. Try to be right with him every second. That'll make

it easier for him than if he's having to fight your weight too. Grip him with your knees and legs, go forward with him or lean a little backward when he's putting on the brakes."

In being glad for Jay, Andy tried to forget her own worries but they were stickily persistent, hovering around like botflies. She could see as plain as print that Blue Smoke's name could never be among the top ten unless they entered a great many shows but school kept her too close to home during the spring and fall when many of the big premium shows were held.

The dude business too was slow. While it meant that

Andy and Jay had more time to ride and school their horse
Andy took it as a personal slur inasmuch as she and Blu
were to have made the Bar D a mecca for dudes. As Jul
wore on, reservations began to come in for Fiesta weeken

"Guess all the Santa Barbara accommodations are booke
up so we're getting some of the overflow." Andy appraise
the situation realistically, knowing it was no indication th
the tide was turning toward them at last.

"What is this Fiesta everyone's talking about all of
sudden?" Jay asked. "Is it something new?"

"You've lived in Los Angeles and never heard of ou
Fiesta? I thought you and your family would probably 'v
been up here for at least one."

"No, they always want to go to the desert, or Baja Cal
fornia, or the redwoods, or—"

"All right, all right. So you've never heard of it! Wel
it isn't new. Santa Barbara's had more than thirty of 'em
It's also called Old Spanish Days and every year durin
August full moon they turn back the clock to when th
city was a Spanish presidio. It opens at the Santa Barba
Mission Wednesday night and Thursday is the most beaut
ful parade—all in costume with beautiful horses and floa
and stuff. Every night there's a pageant and fandangos an
street dancing and a Spanish market place—"

"Whee, it sounds like fun. Do we get to ride in th
parade?"

"Not unless we're in costume," Andy explained and wen
on as if she hadn't been interrupted. "And Saturday there
a stock horse show. I'm going to enter that!"

"Cutting, huh?"

"You bet, and while it isn't quite the same as the Quarter Horse Show it draws horses and riders from all over."

"Let's ride in the parade. I've never been in one. Haven't you got a costume? Or couldn't we rent them?"

"Ye-e-ss, but I don't want to ride Blue when he's going to work the show a couple of days later. Wait though, I've got an idea. Muz, oh, Muz!"

"What is it?"

"I've just had a slick idea that'll maybe get some publicity for the ranch. Jay and I'll get dressed up. I can wear my señorita costume and he can rent a don's outfit. We'll hitch old Sam to our surrey and you sit in the back seat like a Spanish chaperone and rap Jay with your fan if he gets fresh. We'll pretend we're going to be the next bride and groom. For your benefit, Jay, a bride and groom is a central theme for Fiesta because one of the original fiestas was held in connection with a big Spanish wedding." Andy was out of breath from excitement and her rapid-fire speech.

"Jump was wrong. You'd be wasting your time as a lawyer—you have the soul of an advertising expert. That's not a half-bad suggestion either." Mrs. Bard shook her head with astonishment. "Does Sam still know how to wear a harness—and can Jay handle him? Spanish señoritas could ride like centaurs but when they went in carriages they had their own drivers."

"Sure, I think he can. Luis, Luis—"

"She's off, Mrs. Bard. We're as good as riding in that parade right now."

Viva la Fiesta!

Andy's fire-bright eagerness kindled corresponding enthusiasm in the others as one Fiesta plan led to another. After determining that Sam would maintain his gentlemanly mien in harness, the surrey with the fringe on top was washed and polished to restore much of its original elegance.

Mrs. Bard's and Andy's costumes were refurbished by brushing and pressing and Jay contracted for a man's outfit on his next trip to town. He tried it on, preening himself before the mirror like a real Spanish dandy.

"Boy! Am I the gay caballero?" He tilted his head in a characteristic gesture that exactly fit the spirit of the costume, with its black satin lapels, gold braid, colorful sash and the red stripe down the outside trouser seam.

Reservations continued to dribble in by twos and threes until for the first time since the Bar D became a guest ranch it seemed that there would be a full house. Mrs. Bard happily planned for her guests' comfort and pleasure.

"I think we'll have a real Spanish dinner Saturday night after the stock horse show—enchiladas, frijoles, tortillas, tacos. What would you think, Andrea, of our having a dance afterward?"

"It would be super, Muz. Just the right way to end

Fiesta. Of course, I don't know how much dance I'll have left in me after riding Blue in the cutting class, but I'm sure everyone else will. We ought to have more than just square dance music though. 'Viva la Fiesta!' you know."

"That's easy enough. Do you think of anything else we should do?"

"No, probably most of the dudes will spend a lot of time in Santa Barbara on their own. There's the children's parade Saturday too. They can make their own fun the rest of the time."

The Bar D hummed with preparations from morning 'til night. When Andy wasn't working Blue, she was making beds or cleaning rooms. Rosita's niece agreed to come to help throughout Fiesta week, however, and that relieved

Andy and her mother of KP duty. Many of their guests checked in the weekend before Fiesta began. Andy and Jay spent many hours in the saddle wrangling dudes while Blue and Black too came in for their share of work which, with some evening cutting practice, kept them hard and fit. In addition Luis and Jay had several practice sessions with Sam to acquaint the "cowboy from Los Angeles" with the fine art of driving a harness horse.

Thursday morning, parade day, dawned blue and bright with no trace of fog. Luis had put the harness and surrey on the truck the night before so, a few minutes after loading Sam, he headed for Santa Barbara. Mrs. Bard, Jump, Val, Andy and Jay followed in the station wagon. The minute the surrey was unloaded in town they all fell to, twining flowers through the wheels' spokes, running a garland around the top above the fringe, braiding nosegays in Sam's mane and putting a big bouquet of red geraniums on each side of his bridle.

Everywhere was hustle and hurry as riders, carriages and floats were readied for their trip down State Street before the expectant thousands, many of them also in Spanish costume. A flurry of drums heralded the first band's start and one unit after another fed in from side streets. The parade was on.

But for her short hair Andy in a dress of daffodil yellow with a white embroidered shawl might have been a señorita of a hundred years ago, and Jay's authentic costume made him a gallant of presidio days taking his sweetheart and her black-shawled chaperone for a drive. They played their parts well, Andy fluttering her fan and eyelashes at him while businesslike raps from the duenna's fan kept him in his place. A few of their school friends in costume flanked the carriage as outriders and Andy added a little by-play, tossing a flower to one of the boys when Jay was not looking.

"Stop trying to spot your friends in the crowd and keep your mind on that horse a little," Mrs. Bard advised Jay with a particularly businesslike rap that made him wince. "Sam's smart but you're supposed to be the boss."

Their little pantomime pleased the gay spectators who applauded with more than merely polite vigor. Andy gloated every time they passed a loud-speaker that identified them as the entry from the Bar D Guest Ranch.

"There're a lot of people hearing about the ranch today who never knew it existed," Andy whispered to Jay in the guise of a flirtatious sally.

It was mid-afternoon before they reached the disbanding area where Luis met them with the truck. From the moment Jay handed Andy down from the surrey with a courtly gesture, she began looking forward to Saturday's stock horse show. Parade day had been a holiday for Blue but Friday Andy reviewed their basic routine and followed up with a full dress cutting class in the ranch's corral.

"That's enough," she called to Jay who was the hazer, as usual. "He's sharp as a new tack. By this time tomorrow I hope the Bar D will be riding high."

"I wish now I'd entered Black. We couldn't have done any worse than make fools of ourselves."

"True, but the competition's going to be terrific. Blue *has* to be in the money or A. Bard will be insolvent."

That thought tightened her nerves and her resolve to the tension of a steer-held lariat by the time they arrived at the show grounds on Saturday. Eliminations in calf roping, steer stopping and stock horse classes were just concluding, and Andy's heart lurched for fear she should have been there earlier. She hurried to the office where an official reassured her.

"There weren't any cutting horse eliminations, miss. You just have to be on the docket this afternoon when the time comes. Cutting is fifth on the program."

Jay and Luis wanted to look around but Andy was too edgy for sight-seeing. She sat down outside Blue's stall, her back braced against the wall. There was plenty to watch there in the stable area. Horses were being walked up and down to cool them. Others loped easily by, while some raced at full speed only to stop in a stock horse's sliding figure eleven, the hind feet plowing parallel furrows in the dirt.

Andy noticed particularly one man, who sat tall in his saddle, because he was so homely. His face seemed to have been assembled from remnants left over from other faces and the incongruity was completed when he readjusted his Stetson, showing a very white forehead capped with thick, graying hair above his tanned, seamed face.

"Didn't even get a very good color match," Andy thought, smiling inwardly.

The cream-colored Quarter mare he rode was as pretty as her rider was not. Together they looked like a pair of do-ers. A shiver of apprehension ran through Andy lest they be in the cutting horse competition.

"That's one of the handsomest stallions I've seen. I saw you unloading him and he's as pretty as a picture. He's registered, of course." The man had come near enough to open a conversation.

"Yes." Andy did not amplify her monosyllable, going on to a safer topic, the man's own horse. "That's a pretty classy little mare you're riding. Looks like she'd have quite a pick-up and be pretty spry generally."

"Oh, Cream Pitcher does all right. She's always trying anyway."

The girl was stunned. There before her was the top ten's top cutting horse and her owner-rider. Andy knew from reading the horse magazines he was a New Mexico rancher, prominent in stock horse circles, who was taking a bus-man's holiday that season from his well-run ranch to follow the shows.

"Then you're Ross Cameron." Andy's voice sounded thin. She would be showing against them that afternoon.

"Right, and you would be—"

"Blue Smoke and Andy Bard from the Bar D Guest Ranch. Blue, take a bow."

"Sa-ay, the Bar D Guest Ranch, maybe you can help me out. When I got in this morning I discovered there'd been a mix-up in reservations and I don't have a place to stay tonight. It's 'No Vacancy' all over Santa Barbara for Fiesta. Suppose you folks would have an extra bed and a place for The Pitcher?"

"No, I don't think— Oh, yes, we would too," she amended, remembering Pop's cabin, "but it isn't very ultra.

You realize too that if you beat us this afternoon you run the risk of tacks in your bed?"

"Anything better than a stall is all right with me. I'll follow you home after the show."

As soon as Jay and Luis returned, the trio strolled over to the chuck wagon for lunch although Andy's butterflies left little room for food. She saddled up immediately afterward and joined the milling riders, all of whom were warming up their horses for one event or another.

Lots were drawn shortly for the cutters' order of appearance and Andy drew fourth, dead center of the seven entries. She paid little attention to the first four events, walking Blue constantly until the preceding class was in the arena. Then she took him out where the eliminations had been held and cantered him in slow, short circles.

"All cutting horses in the arena, please. Let's get 'em in here promptly. Lots more classes to come."

With the other riders Andy rode through the gate, her right hand in her pocket, its fingers tightly crossed for luck. The horse to win that class would have to be extra good. Every other horse there had been a winner and from the tips of their ears to the frogs of their hoofs they were all real cow horses.

When the first contestant rode out to do his best with the flighty cattle, Andy ranged Blue into the group of nonworkers where she found herself beside Ross Cameron.

"Who's hazing for you?" he asked. "Then how about me?" he continued at a shake of her head.

Andy flashed an affirmative smile and nodded vigorously as the second rider set to work. This was more than she dared to ask but was exactly what she had hoped for. She was confident that Blue was good enough to hold his own even when showing with the top horse but she could never have brought herself to ask Cameron to haze for her.

Both the second and third horses turned in creditable performances. Andy squared her jaw and her shoulders and rode out when her name was called. Blue's neck was low, his ears set forward as he took the herd's measure. He sauntered forward with complete unconcern until the cattle swirled around him like a red river, Andy's eyes darting from one to another. A scrawny one shyly burrowed into the herd for protection.

"That's for us, Blue. Get him out."

The reins told Blue more than Andy's words as he eased around the critter, pushing him closer and closer to the rim, then into the open without the others noticing. The red waves closed in behind. Blue's rump just barely cleared the herd when the steer wheeled and wanted to get back in, but Blue said "No!" The animal ducked the other way, but the horse still barred his path. Like a fencer with his back to a wall Blue parried the steer's every thrust.

Blue blocked one feint after another and despite the steer's stubborn resistance he was forced back step by step as a stronger swordsman sweeps his adversary before him. The gap between Blue's hindquarters and the herd widened slowly. Cameron sat his horse alertly, ready to head off any retreat but Andy's shy one never turned to run.

She held up her hand to indicate she was going back to pick out a different animal. Time was running out but she wanted one that Blue could work faster. Right at the edge of the herd she spotted one that the second rider had just started when the whistle blew. At Andy's direction Blue slipped him out in the clear.

Unable to run out because of the hazer the animal bolted crossways of the arena, Blue matching him step for step with the reins flapping loosely. Finding escape cut off at that side the critter cut back. Blue was mad clear through that his mastery should be disputed. He pinned his ears tight to his head and bared his teeth to discourage further insubordination as he sidestepped the arena's width with the speed and neatness of a dancer gliding across the floor.

Just as Blue deflected the steer's desperate lunge to gain the herd's haven the whistle blew. Andy slapped Blue's shoulder approvingly.

"Holy Toledo! What a horse," Ross Cameron cried as they rode back into line. "How come I've never heard of him before? I should think he'd be cleaning up everywhere. The Pitcher'll have to go some to beat that score."

"Well, it wouldn't break my heart if she couldn't." Andy grinned happily. "You want me to haze for you?"

"I wish you could but before I found out what a blue whirlwind your horse is, I asked Joe over there. Thanks though."

The only other girl entry showed between Andy's and Cameron's turns but after seeing her horse work Andy felt there was nothing to fear there. The Pitcher sneaked quietly into the herd and brought out an animal that proved as slippery as a greased pig but the mare was a match for him. Speed was her undoing, however, for she headed him off with such a rush she overshot a half length and though she made a quick recovery without losing the steer, Andy saw the judge mark his score pad.

One more contestant and the match was over. Following a pause for final computation of the scores, the announcer who had turned away to confer with the judges picked up the mike to give the winners. Andy's head reeled with sudden dizziness and she found that she had been holding her breath too long.

"The winner of this interesting class, ladies and gentlemen, is Blue Smoke, owned and ridden by Andy Bard of the Bar D Guest Ranch. Second, by only three points, is Cream Pitcher, the well-known mare, owned and ridden by Ross Cameron."

Andy grabbed the saddle horn to steady herself. Blue had won. He had beaten the top horse at her own game. Pinwheels of exuberance flashed through Andy's head and she fell over on Blue's neck to hug him.

"Can't think of a nicer person to lose to."

At Cameron's words of congratulation, she straightened up in the saddle.

"Thanks mucho. No tacks in your bed tonight."

As soon as the stock horse show was over deft, quick-moving men and women loaded horses into trailers and trucks to the accompaniment of hoofs drumming on plank floors, homesick whinnies, challenging neighs and shouted banter and congratulations.

"Does Cream Pitcher ever really pitch?" Blue had been put in his trailer and Andy's question was prompted by seeing Cameron toss the rope over the mare's neck to let her walk in the trailer alone.

"Not now, but she gave me some pretty rough rides a
first—until we understood each other," he answered as he
and Luis fastened the tailgate bolts. "Boy, that bed is going
to be really welcome. You're sure there's room for me?"
Cameron stretched his long frame that already seemed so
relaxed Andy wondered that he didn't fall to pieces.

"Oh, sure, but to be doubly sure I phoned Muz. There'
one thing I forgot to tell you though. I hope you like Mex-
ican food. We're having our final Fiesta dinner and old-
fashioned dance tonight. You'll have music to go to sleep
to."

"A dance? Who's going to sleep? How about the first
one with me?"

"She can't. It's mine." Jay spoke up truculently. He had
been necessarily on the sidelines all day and until this opening had had to be content with glowering.

"Too bad. Maybe the second—or the third," the older
man temporized as Jay's dark look only darkened. .

"We'll work one in. Muz is really a better dancer than
I am anyway. Come on, let's get going."

An hour later the two pick-ups and trailers drew up at
the Bar D. Had Blue lost that day, Andy would have been
too tired to look forward to the dance but his thrilling
victory put wings on her toes. She romped through caring
for the horse and changed into her Fiesta dress for dinner

Mrs. Bard in her black Spanish costume and lace mantilla
was the personification of the gracious hostess as she moved
about seeing to everyone's comfort and pleasure. When the
musicians struck up the lively Spanish dance, *Chiapanegas*

Jay and Andy joined in enthusiastically as did Muz and Ross Cameron.

Mrs. Bard's face was delicately flushed and in her gay Fiesta mood she might have been just a señorita herself instead of a señora with the cares of a ranch and three children. Andy's feet followed where Jay led but her mind followed her mother and partner as the girl strove to recall some half-forgotten memory.

"She looks like she's swallowed a neon tube—like the night the Whitcombs' friend came up for our square dance." Right on the heels of this discovery came another. "Why, she likes to have a good time as much as I do!"

The dance was a whirlwind of gaiety for everyone, guests and residents. Their shouted "Viva la Fiesta!" at midnight was a knell for that celebration but it also held eager anticipation for the next.

·19·

I Challenge

The Bar D lost its entire guest list the next day with the exception of Ross Cameron who stayed on for a few days to rest Cream Pitcher before resuming her campaign for cutting horse honors. He accommodated himself to the ranch routine so easily he hardly seemed like a guest.

He and Luis talked cattle and ranching, Jump enlisted his aid in persuading Mrs. Bard it was time to replace the boy's gentle horse with one more spirited, while Val renamed her favorite kitten Ross. Andy found herself pouring out the whole story of Blue's quasi-ownership to the newcomer and asking his advice.

"I'd been wondering why you didn't show him in the Quarter Horse Show. Thought maybe you were scared out."

"Not me, although every time he wins something and his name gets into print I'm plenty scared. If anyone claimed him, I wouldn't be able to do a thing and 'for want of a paper the horse would be lost.' Do you have any bright ideas? We've used all of ours up."

"Nary a one." Ross scratched his head. "Seems as if you've gone about as far as you can go. Say, not to change the subject, of course, but when are you going to give The Pitcher a chance to even the score?"

"Not for quite a while, I guess. The Ventura Fair in early October is about the only one I can make, but Muz promised that Blue and I can go to that since it's not so awfully far and I won't have to miss school—at least not much. You planning to be there?"

"Yes, I think I will—if I can put up here for a little while before and after. Don't want The Pitcher to get too tired, you know."

This seemed like a strange stipulation for a mare that had trailered as much as the cream, but a guest was a guest. Andy took it as a compliment for the Bar D that he was enjoying the present lay-over enough to want to come back.

"Don't see why you couldn't. We're never booked solid at that time of year—" nor any other, she silently admitted.

His last night there he got up from the supper table promptly.

"You kids behave yourselves tonight while we're gone. I'm taking my hostess to town to the movies."

"That's news to me," Mrs. Bard protested. "Why, I haven't been to a movie in months—maybe years."

"Past time you did then. Don't change or try to fix up. You're pretty enough now."

Such masterful tactics overwhelmed the young ones as well as their mother. Before they could blink twice the car bearing Mrs. Bard and Mr. Cameron disappeared along the curving driveway.

"Man of action, isn't he?" Jay commented.

"I'm glad. Muz hasn't had any fun to speak of since—I guess since Daddy died," Andy reflected.

"I think he's sweet on Muz." Val nodded sagely to emphasize her point.

"That a girl for you. Always getting romantic notions," Jump scoffed with brotherly scorn. "Ross hasn't got time for women."

Andy wasn't so sure and often during the evening she found her mind wandering from their game of spit-in-the-ocean. The movie-goers had not returned by the time the quartet disbanded to go to bed, Andy keeping a big-sisterly eye on the process. Much later she awoke to hear her mother tiptoeing in, and went sleepily into the hall to talk to her.

"Good grief! What happened? Did you have car trouble?" Andy blinked like an owl in the bright light.

"Oh, no," her mother denied. "We were hungry after the show so we dropped in at a place where there was an orchestra and we danced a while. Sorry to have disturbed you, dear. Now skip back to bed."

It was nearly noon the next day before Ross Cameron had packed his things, loaded Cream Pitcher and was ready to depart.

"Adios, until October," he called as the pick-up rolled forward but Andy, who was on the alert, felt that he was actually saying it to her mother.

Summer's end was pleasantly dull. Andy and Jay spent as many hours on horseback as they possibly could, for the latter faced returning to his Los Angeles home and school. His heart was heavy at the prospect of leaving Black Magic behind although Mr. Whitcomb considered board-

ing the horse at the Bar D instead of selling him a handsome concession.

"There'll be vacations when you can come up and ride,
and maybe a long weekend once in a while," Andy con-
soled. "I'll take good care of him and—and if I should lose
Blue I can ride Black Magic all the time."

"What a gruesome thought. What brought that up?"

"I don't know, but it's always a possibility."

"Don't let it get you down. I'd be glad to have Black
get daily work but not *that* way. Say, you've never told
me what you're going to do with all that money you won
for first in the show. Why don't you get a car now that
you have a driver's license?"

"Well, I have to have entry money for the Ventura
show."

"That won't use more'n a tenth of it. Gonna put the
rest in your sock?"

"No, I have plans. I'll tell you later."

"Supposin' I'm not here."

"I write English if you can read it."

With that Jay had to be content, for he had not wheedled
the secret out of her before he had to go back to the city.
Andy was almost glad to return to school, for it meant that
October and the Ventura Fair and Rodeo was that much
nearer.

The latter half of September she practiced Blue's cutting
right after school but for the week intervening between
daylight saving's end and their Ventura appearance she
worked under Jay's floodlights. Again Andy was grateful
for them as the approaching event was held in the evening

under artificial light so Blue needed to become reaccustomed to the different conditions.

"I should think Cream Pitcher and her boss ought to be getting here pretty quick," Andy mused aloud one evening. "The Fair starts in a few days."

"Yes, but the cutting classes aren't the first day," Mrs. Bard pointed out. Andy was surprised to find her mother so up-to-date. "He'll likely get here tomorrow."

Sure enough, his pick-up and trailer were parked by the stable, Cameron and her mother standing near it, when Andy came home from school. She was too glad to see him to wonder at her mother's sixth sense.

"Hello, how's the top cutting horse and her owner?"

"I wouldn't know. The Pitcher dropped to second place last week."

"She did! That's terrible. Oh, I'm so sorry."

Andy's sympathy was real.

"Take it easy. Why should you feel so bad? I'll admit I'm not cheering about it myself, but I'd hardly expect you to get so cut up about it."

The girl's measured glance took them both in before she spoke.

"Well, I've had a scheme in the back of my head since the Fiesta show. Blue and I can't get to enough shows to make a dent in this top ten rating, so I'd been thinking that if you and The Pitcher came out tops after the Cow Palace show, Blue and I would challenge you to a special match—for charity or something. It wouldn't alter the standings at all, but Blue and the Bar D would get a lot of publicity out of it and—"

"Andy, Andy, the ranch is getting along all right. When are you going to stop worrying about making a go of the dude angle?"

"When we have to turn people away because we're full up."

"You know, that's a pretty sharp idea you've got there." Cameron was so engrossed with Andy's idea he hardly heard the mother and daughter exchange. "It ought to create quite a stir in cutting horse—or all stock horse circles. How'd you figure to run it?"

"That I wasn't too sure about, but I did read somewhere about a match in which each horse had to cut out several head of fresh stock. We could hold it here, for instance, or some neutral place if it matters, but all the cattle would have to be fresh and not worked before."

"Blue'd give a good account of himself. The only reason he isn't one of the top ten is that you can't show him enough. It's a date, if The Pitcher is grand champion at the Cow Palace next month, maybe even if she isn't—I can't think of a cutting horse man who wouldn't be sport enough to welcome that sort of deal."

This encouragement so stimulated Andy that she was tireless in getting Blue ready for the Ventura show. It was essential that he make a superlative showing that weekend for her challenge to be taken seriously by anyone other than Cameron. There were two classes for Blue, one the heavyweight, the other the open class that all horses could enter, for a sizable fee. Cream Pitcher and Cameron were entered in the lightweight and open classes, the latter being their only chance to even their score with Blue.

Had they been in the heavyweight class they would h
succeeded, not through any fault of Blue's but because
Andy's vanity. With some of her prize money she
bought a whole new outfit that to a thread fulfilled
westerner's love of color: slate blue saddle pants and
to complement Blue's own color, a red shirt with w
yoke, cuffs and piping, and red and white boots.

Andy's work on Blue had paid off and he was in
form when she rode him into the brightly lighted arc
For the first time since she had been showing him he fre
a little while waiting his turn so when his chance came
gave it all he had. Andy picked a salty old steer and h
didn't miss a step. Back and forth, up and back, t
dodged and charged while Andy clung desperately to
saddle to counteract her new pants' slickness on the p
ished saddle.

Blue dashed to head off the steer's sudden lunge, pivo
his back legs halfway under his belly and within a s
second was headed the other way as the critter chan
directions. Not Andy. She had been snapped out of
saddle and rode thin air to the ground where she hit w
a resounding thump.

The reins fell across the horn so rider or no rider B
knew that steer needed putting in his place and he was j
the horse who proposed to do it. Andy had no breath j
then to call him if she would have. Regaining her brea
she sat spellbound in the dirt watching Blue play the st
like a good dog herds sheep. Several seconds of lightn
work later the heaving Hereford halted and Blue plac

himself between the critter and the herd, shaking his head menacingly while he dared the other to make a break for it.

Andy arose. Her new blue pants seemed to have a big brown patch on the seat where she hit the dirt. She slapped at it tenderly as she limped over and caught Blue. The spectators cheered wildly, whistled, stamped, to show their enjoyment of this unscheduled entertainment.

The announcer himself was amused. "Ladies and gentlemen, any cutting horse man will tell you that a good horse enjoys his work as much as the rider. One or two have on

occasion worked without a bridle to prove it, but you have just seen a remarkable exhibition of a self-working horse. Of course, that does not alter the cutting horse association rule that disqualifies an entry if the rider is unseated."

Andy was mortified at her part in the "remarkable exhibition" but remounted with what nonchalance she could muster. She was doubly chagrined that it should happen when Muz was present. Meeting her after the class her mother seemed quite unruffled by Andy's misfortune.

" 'Pride goeth before a fall' all right. You proved it."

"Yeah, and what a fall," Andy admitted ruefully. "My sit-down-on still stings."

Andy left her new finery at home the next night and dressed inconspicuously in working cowboy attire. As an added safeguard she took a damp sponge to wet the saddle seat, dimming a little of its luster and increasing its friction. The open cutting class was with one exception the combined light and heavyweight classes. Though Blue's ambitious owner knew he would have to be good to win it, she also knew that if he had the snap and zip of the night before he couldn't miss.

In drawing for turns she took second but this did not disturb her too much. This was Blue's night. She felt it in every pore and corpuscle. Blue thought so too, for he practically swaggered through their warm-up and entering the arena Andy could feel the strut in his short, quick step.

The first contestant made a good, honest showing but when the roan's turn came he outdid himself. Andy's sixth sense for picking good stock was never better and she cut out one really rambunctious one that Blue played fast and close.

His rider's dress was different but Blue had not changed clothes and the spectators, many of them repeats from the night before, made him their favorite and cheered him on uproariously. This tumult reminded the horse of his race-track days which spurred him to greater efforts. When the whistle blew to end their turn Andy wore her poker face but inside she too was cheering. Blue had been invincible.

"That'll give you and Cream Pitcher something to shoot at," she said to Cameron as they changed places, his turn coming next.

"Holy Toledo! I'll say it will. Blue's unbeatable tonight I think."

Andy's unexpressed hope and Cameron's voiced opinion proved correct. Blue again bested The Pitcher who came in second. The announcer finished naming the four winners. The gate opened and cutting horses and their riders drove the cattle back to the pens, but Andy rode over and, drawing a letter out of her pocket, she handed it up to the announcer in his tower. There was a long silence from the loudspeaker instead of the usual chatter that is an announcer's stock in trade. Then Andy heard what she had been waiting for.

"Listen to this, friends. I have just been handed this letter and I'll read it to you word for word:

'To the National Cutting Horse Champion's Owner— whoever you turn out to be next month at the Cow Palace: My horse Blue and I can't get around to a lot of shows on account of my going to school so he'll never have a chance

to hit the Top Ten but I'm sure he's every bit as good
any horse showing. To prove this isn't just talk, I challer
you and your horse to a match in which each horse cuts
at least fifteen fresh two-year-old heifers. The proceeds fr
this match (to be held at a place and time convenient
both of us) can go to any charity you want to name.

'I am sending this challenge officially to all cutting ho
associations but am presenting it here tonight to give eve1
one plenty of advance notice.

'P.S. How about Armistice Day or Thanksgiving wee
end? I won't have to go to school then.'

"Folks, it's signed by that great little girl who just show
'em all how it's done right here tonight. There she is no
Andy Bard and Blue Smoke of the Bar D Guest Ranc
take a bow. Well, how d'ya like that?"

They liked it, judging by the thunderclap of applau
that died away to the excited buzzing of many convers
tions. Andy had provided another thrill for riders and spe
tators alike and the buzzing went on and on and on, arou1
the stables, over telephone and telegraph wires, wherev
two horsemen met.

·20·

A Losing Victory

During the five weeks that separated the Ventura show from the Cow Palace finals of the cutting horse championship Andy's mailbag proved that a match would be a big success. Several owners of high-ranking horses wrote, each one saying that he would be glad to accept her challenge should his horse win the coveted national title.

Many others wrote to express their enthusiasm for such a match and to ask that they be informed of the time and place. At first Andy's heart pounded heavily at every strange envelope she opened but as time went by and no one questioned Blue's ownership her taut nerves relaxed. If Pop's son was going to claim Blue, he would have done so long since.

Any one of Andy's days would have made the proverbial one-armed paperhanger look like a loafer. Blue's exercise and schooling could not be neglected, all her letters had to be answered properly yet school went on just the same. She was frantic with pressure. For a while it seemed that nothing would get done right until one night the idea of doubling up came to her.

The next day she talked to the commercial subjects teacher and persuaded her that the class might well be working on real rather than fictional letters. Thenceforth the advanced typing group served as her secretary. The more important letters Andy answered personally but the general queries as to where and when were neatly copied from a form letter Andy had provided.

Unexpected help came from another quarter. Cameron and Cream Pitcher had departed to attend another show a few days after Ventura but he did not stay away long.

"I decided The Pitcher needed a little lay-off. She's going sort of sour from so much showing, so this seemed like a good place for a little vacation until Cow Palace time."

As the days raced by Andy wondered whose vacation it was, his or The Pitcher's. The mare was worked every day to be sure as he and Andy alternately cut and hazed for each other but many an evening he and Mrs. Bard drove off to the movies or dancing or a concert. Andy had never seen her mother in a gayer mood. As the October days went by Andy watched her chance. She was getting ready for bed one night and heard her mother humming as she moved about her room.

"Muz," Andy called out as if the idea had just occurred to her, "let's go up to the Cow Palace too. Rosita can look after Jump and Val for a few days."

"Whatever put such an outlandish notion in your head? Of course, we can't go up to San Francisco."

"It'd be fun to see Ross and The Pitcher in that cutting class—and I guess everyone has a wonderful time there," Andy said in an off-hand way.

"They'll just have to have a good time without our help then. Goodness knows, you're not getting much out of school now with your head so full of horses, but at least your body is there."

Andy knew when she had to take "no" for an answer and desisted. She had, in fact, had little hope from the start but was determined to try. Her mother's refusal grew harder and harder to bear, however, as Ross prepared to leave, notwithstanding his promise to act as her agent in arranging the match.

He was a man of his word too, phoning the Bar D after every go-round to keep them posted. While he always seemed to call when Andy was away, her mother relayed the information to her so Andy had to be content. He had seen to it that all cutting horse owners received a copy of her challenge and now she could only wait.

The night of the finals Andy could not sit still and roamed the house like a strange cat while she watched the clock like a mouse. A dozen times she asked her mother if she didn't think it was time Ross phoned but the black instrument remained stubbornly silent. Jump and Val had long since gone to bed but Andy and Mrs. Bard kept the vigil. Eleven, eleven-thirty, twelve the clock showed.

"Something's gone wrong or he'd surely have called by now. Maybe he won't phone after all." Andy's drumming fingertips stopped sharply at such a thought.

"If he said he would, he will."

Mrs. Bard's statement of faith was no sooner spoken than the phone shrilled its reward. Andy jumped for it.

"Hello, Ross. Who won? What happened?"

"Slim Simmons from Arizona on his seal brown gelding,

Coffee Grounds, won the show and enough points to cin
the championship—"

"And will he agree to a match with Blue?"

"He wasn't very anxious to, said he'd never heard
your horse before news of your challenge got around. P
sides he wants to get home—"

"He's got to!" Andy wailed. "Tell him—"

"I did." It was Ross's turn to interrupt. "Now hold
a minute so I can finish. He didn't want to but I talked fa
and long to him so he finally agreed to it if Armistice D
is all right with you. That's just next Monday but he'll
going home through Southern California and will work
in."

"Where, Ross? And what about stock?"

"That's all taken care of too. All Slim agreed to cut
fifteen head. The manager of the Squared Circle Du
Ranch is up here and he offered his place and his cattle
it's there pretty close to the Bar D, isn't it?"

"Yeah, just a few miles. In fact, there's where Blue c
his first show critter. What about judges and—and ever
thing?" Things were moving so fast Andy scrabbled
keep pace.

"That's all right too. This is the best place in the wor
to work out such a deal because everyone—everyone exce
the Bards, that is—who is interested in cutting horses
here. Get those postcards out to people who have writte
to ask about it. I'll be there tomorrow night and tell yo
all about it. Your mother there?"

Mrs. Bard took the phone that Andy relinquished. H
head whirled. Have to get the typing class busy on tho

postcard notifications and—and what else? Ross seemed to have the situation well in hand. Blue was at his peak.

Andy set a new record between the bus stop and the house the next afternoon after school but Ross had not yet arrived. She went to change her clothes only to hear his car and trailer pulling up the driveway. Her costume half and half, school and home, she hurried out to meet him.

"I'd have been here sooner but people kept shoving these at me." He dropped a sheaf of checks and reservations in Mrs. Bard's hands. "Well, it looks like quite a clambake, folks. Everyone who can possibly get here will be here. The Squared Circle's guest list was full too before Mr. Trent left San Francisco and I reckon these'll give you a full house."

"How'd you ever get Simmons to agree to the match?" Andy asked, wide-eyed with admiration of Ross's persuasive powers.

"I used every logical argument I could. When they failed, I talked to him in a language he could understand."

"He isn't a logical type, eh?" Andy laughed, missing the point entirely.

"Ross, you shouldn't have—" Mrs. Bard's reproof was lost in his reply.

"Let's say he's the practical type. Well, are you and Blue all ready for the big day?"

"All we need now is the day itself."

That week bolted past like a frightened horse, the Bar D folks dragging along as they tried to keep things right side up. Andy was so occupied with her horse she was little help on anything else so Mrs. Bard, Rosita and Luis worked feverishly to get ready for the influx of guests. Ross too helped when not busy working out the details of the match.

Friday night came and with it Jay and all the Whitcombs unannounced, so the Bards doubled up, letting them have Andy's and Val's rooms while Jay moved in with Jump. Saturday brought most of the guests so Sunday afternoon the Bar D gave an old California barbecue for their guests, those at the Squared Circle, the three judges and friends.

Andy met Slim Simmons for the first time, Ross having concluded the final arrangements for her. The girl immediately liked the lanky, slow-spoken westerner who was cut from the same piece of goods Ross was. One look at Blue Smoke and the national champion's owner was more impressed.

"Say, he looks like quite a piece of horse. Old Coffee Grounds and I may be kept pretty busy tomorrow."

"That's what Blue and I aim to do. I'm convinced he's as good as the best; tomorrow I hope to convince you."

"*If* you can," Slim amended with a soft laugh.

Everyone but the Bar D's own guests left by nightfall when only a lingering trace of wood smoke and roast beef remained in the clear, chilly air. As Andy and Jay walked toward the stables to "tuck Blue in bed," as she put it, she shivered uncomfortably.

"Catching cold? Here, take my jacket," Jay urged with the combined solicitude of a prizefighter's manager and a protective friend.

"No, I'm not cold, but I feel uneasy, sort of as though someone was staring at me."

She was startled by Jay's burst of laughter. "I've got

news for you—you were stared at all afternoon, everyone wondering how to place their bets."

"Bets!"

"Sure, you don't think a bunch of horsemen could let a thing like this pass without having a little money riding on one horse or the other, do you?"

"I suppose not, but I didn't mean that. It's like in a restaurant when you feel you have to look around and you see someone looking at you. That's the way I felt all afternoon."

"Aw-w, you've just got the jitters."

"You can say that again."

Andy wondered whether or not she would be able to sleep but even sharing her mother's bed was no hindrance. She blacked out with the light when Mrs. Bard switched it off. Opening her eyes to bright sunlight Andy thought for a moment it was the light still on but the next instant she knew it was her day of days and bounded out of bed.

The swift current she herself had set in motion picked her up and whirled her along until it dropped her at the Squared Circle all ready to mount Blue. All nervousness and worry dropped away as soon as she settled into the saddle. From this vantage point the size of the crowd astonished her.

Riding Blue toward the gateway she saw a familiar face and she half-checked Blue only to discover it was a stranger she had never met before. There was a curious resemblance, however, to someone she had known and she puzzled over it for the moment or two it took to ride into the large, fenced arena that covered almost an acre.

This match was different from their previous contests in that each animal cut from the bunch must be moved to the far end of the arena. There cowboys held this smaller but constantly growing "cut" while each contestant alternately added an animal to it. Both Slim and Andy had a hazer standing by, but his work was not important since the sole aim of the contest was to move the cattle one by one from the original herd to the new bunch at the opposite end.

Slim, who won the coin toss, elected to work second. Doing a few salaams to Lady Luck, Andy moved Blue toward the large, milling herd. First turn was a definite disadvantage this time since the cattle were young, flighty heifers.

With instinctive caution the horse sauntered up to the cattle as if he were one himself and Andy cut off their first animal to take down to the other end. She was a wily one, but Blue countered her at every turn. At last she had no choice but to give in and go, bawling her protests vehemently.

Slim's first critter was more amenable and after a quick turn or two trotted docilely down the fence to join the cut without giving Coffee Grounds much chance to show off. Andy's second choice was fairly co-operative almost to the other end, but then she made a break for it. Blue wheeled like lightning and his racetrack speed paid off. Halfway back to the herd he caught and turned her.

"Wow! That was a close one, guy. Let one get away and our goose is probably cooked."

Working alternately Andy and Slim whittled away at

the herd, no two heifers behaving the same. Andy and Blue were forcing their unwilling sixth from one end to the other. She stopped midway of the fence line. During the split second Blue took to read her mind Andy glanced through the mesh fencing and saw the same man she had noticed earlier.

Her head reeled with recognition. It was Pop—no, not Pop as she had known him but Pop maybe twenty years ago. His son! Come to claim Blue. Then Andy recalled having seen that same vaguely familiar face at the Fiesta show. Had she seen it at Ventura too? She was too confused to remember.

Before she could regather her wits the heifer hightailed across the arena. Blue turned too, quicker than thought, but Andy's thoughts were elsewhere. She wobbled in the saddle, off balance as a sack of sand. Here Blue's tremendous power showed itself, for despite his rider's weight being clear off center he stayed with the heifer and turned her.

Nothing but Andy's instinctive leg grip prevented her from hitting the dirt and forfeiting the match then and there. It jarred her enough physically and mentally to recall her to her senses so she and Blue soon put the critter in her place.

Slim and Coffee Grounds went out for their turn and Andy thought fast to figure out a course of action. Her first impulse was to deliberately lose the match. Then Blue would not look so desirable. He would in fact look rather ridiculous. So too would she and Ross and all of Blue's

backers who were foolish enough to pit a newcomer lik
the roan against a recognized champion.

No, she couldn't throw the match. It would be unfair—
even downright dishonest. Why, Ross must have money o
this match, she realized in a flash. He had probably put u
a purse on the side. That was the language Slim could un

derstand. She hadn't understood plain English. Her fac
burned with excitement and embarrassment. Blue deserve
to win too. The miles and miles he had walked and can
tered, the hours he had spent in training were not to b
thrown away on an impulse.

"Miss Bard, it's your go now."

From the judge's tone Andy was sure that was not th
first time he had called to her. Her start of surprise move
Blue forward but she was still so confused he was the guid
ing force. They were almost to the herd before Andy
snapped out of her daze. If Blue was to win, and now tha
she saw the full picture he had to, she must wake up an

ride. She wondered uneasily how much her lapse might have cost them in points. Whatever it was, she resolved they would be their last demerits. She was riding to win, come what may!

Blue felt her altered attitude and he perked up. From then on they became an unbeatable team, never making a wrong move. Coffee Grounds' thirteenth heifer was his unlucky one. She had played him back and forth two or three times until he was mad clear through. She turned tail and shot back toward the herd, Coffee Grounds after her like a juggernaut, but he was overzealous and went beyond her, not far enough to lose control but enough to make Slim rein in.

Their margin of loss was close when the last critter was cut and the totals added up. Blue had successfully covered up Andy's brief lapse but there was no covering up Coffee Grounds' error in judgment. The heat of the match over, Andy was too numb with dread to move. She heard the cheers, accepted Slim's astonished congratulations, but was incapable of action as well as incapable of thinking what to do. She knew that the instant she reached the gate that man would be there to reach out for Blue's bridle. Through the fence she saw Ross and Muz, their faces alight with excitement.

"Get around to the gate before I come out, will you?"

"What's the matter, Andy? Success too much for you? Feeling a little sick to your stomach?" Ross hooted.

"Andrea, what's wrong? You do look sick."

"I'm all right. Just get over there quick before I come out."

Her strange behavior sobered them and she watched them push through the crowd around the gate. She wanted to run away, to hide from that face, but she knew it was no use. A sorrier victor than Andy never rode out of an arena. She turned toward the gate as though she faced a firing squad.

"This is it, Blue, boy. You won but it's a losing victory."

·21·

Waking Nightmare

Slim and Coffee Grounds had already ridden out but the crowd waiting at the gate to cheer the victor surged around Andy and her horse. Jay, whose family had let him stay on, though they had to leave as soon as the contest ended, was the first to reach her but her expression warned him of trouble ahead. Many there were friends and acquaintances from the Valley while others she recognized from shows she had been in. She tried to fix her face into one suitable for the winner of a hard, hot contest.

It was no use. She saw the man jostling his way toward her through the massed people while only a few steps behind and unaware of the impending crisis, Ross was opening a path for Mrs. Bard. Andy was still horseman enough to keep an eye on her mount who was being shoved and buffeted by his well-wishers, but she sat hunched in the saddle, awaiting the blow.

"I'm Albert Reed. Guess you know why I'm here. I've come for the horse."

Andy nodded mutely. Not so Ross who was close enough to hear Reed's words.

"Well, I'm sure glad to meet you, Mr. Reed. I've been wanting to buy this horse for a long time but didn't know where to get in touch with you. What'll you take for him?"

"He ain't for sale. I've got other plans for him. We kin jus' as well put him in my trailer right here."

"Hold on, I'm afraid it won't be quite that simple. He's been held under a court order so it will take the court's permission to release him."

The people had begun to drift away but they swarmed back at this hint of drama. During this exchange Andy had been looking the man over and from his untidy hair to his rumpled clothes she did not like one thing about him. Contrasting him with Pop almost brought her to tears but strong pressure on her boot by Jay helped her control her emotions. Mrs. Bard was loath to provide further entertainment for the crowd and spoke up.

"This is no place to talk. You'd better come home with us tonight and we'll talk it all over. You'll want to get your father's things anyway—though goodness knows, he had little enough."

"I'll say I will." Reed spoke truculently, his tone implying that unless he was careful he would be cheated out of them. "Well, all right, if you've got room for two. My wife's with me."

"Blue's tired and needs looking after. I'll take him to the trailer." Andy's first thought, as always, was for her horse but the newcomer suspected trickery.

"I'll just come along too. Nice animal, isn't he?" Reed's eyes gleamed when he looked at Blue's rounded perfection but Andy felt sure he saw, not the horse, but a dollar sign.

"Where'll you put 'em, Muz?" the girl asked on the way home. "The cottage?"

"No, indeed. If the cabin was good enough for Pop it's good enough for his son. They'll make out, if we put another cot in there for Fuzzy Hair. Besides, we don't know anything about them. They may be criminals for all we know—that letter of Pop's didn't make Albert sound very desirable."

Andy measured her mother's dislike of the man and his cheap little wife by Mrs. Bard's disinterest in her guests' comfort as well as this derogatory remark—the first Andy had ever heard her make.

"I'm glad we've got a man in the house." Val's eyes were kitten-wide.

"So am I," her mother agreed but Andy was too sunk in misery to worry about her own safety.

Supper was the uneasiest meal Andy had ever tried to eat. The Reeds' presence drained all the joy and triumph out of Andy's sensational showing that afternoon and limited table conversation to "Please pass the butter," or "Thank you, no more potatoes." No one had time to talk anyway. Every Bar D brain was in high gear in one last, desperate attempt to solve the registration papers' mystery, but not an eye gleamed with hope.

Tension increased when the farcical meal was finished and they all settled down in the living room to discuss the situation. First of all, Ross renewed his offer for Blue but it was refused again. Andy's sixth sense caught the feeling that Reed already had a high-paying buyer. He pressed his advantage.

"Well, the first thing to get straightened out tonight is the horse's winnings while you had him. I figure he made close to a thousand dollars. A check is all right—I can tell you're honest."

Andy and the other Bards were speechless with surprise and anger at the man's effrontery, but Ross's calm acceptance of such bare-faced extortion left them gasping.

"Yes, that's so, Blue has taken in a little prize money. I'm glad you brought it up."

While Cameron figured swiftly on the back of an envelope Andy saw Reed lick his lips greedily. She wondered hysterically where she could raise the money.

"Andy, think of any other prizes Blue won besides these?" Cameron ticked off one show after another where Blue had been in the money.

"There was that ladies' race I rode him to first in," she replied dully, too dazed to struggle further if Ross had deserted them.

"That wouldn't count. Pop was alive then and the money went to him." Ross at least disallowed this sum. "You think of any others, Reed?"

"No, no, that's just fine." He massaged his hands eagerly.

"Then, let me see," Cameron murmured to himself as he figured rapidly, "that will cut down your bill quite a little. You will owe Mrs. Bard just— Well, call it an even five hundred dollars."

"I owe her?" Reed's yelp was that of a hurt cur. "What kind of arithmetic is that?"

"Just common sense is all. If she is not to have the horse's earnings, you will be liable for the horse's board for eight-

een months plus a small fee for Miss Bard's time and training which, as you know, made the horse a second-to-none
cutting horse."

The Bards breathed again but shallowly as they awaited
Reed's reply. For once he was speechless so their champion
made another suggestion.

"Of course, they have had the use of the horse and it
may be that Mrs. Bard and her daughter will not want to
press their claim. In that case, it would be better to just
call it a draw and no money changes hands at all. Is that
satisfactory to all of you?"

Everyone nodded agreement, each one trying to hide the
relief such a compromise afforded.

"You might as well give me the horse's papers tonight,"
Reed blustered to cover his defeat. "Then that'll be out of
the way."

"We can't. We don't have them."

"Don't have 'em? You must have 'em. The horse was
registered and the old man'd never be careless with anything like that. You're hiding 'em."

Reed's eyes glittered suspiciously as his glance darted
from one to the other.

"Not likely," Andy said bitterly. "Pop told me just before he died the horse was to be mine, but we haven't ever
been able to find the papers. You're lucky we don't have
them, or we'd also have proof that Blue *is* mine."

This angle cooled Reed off perceptibly, that being the
last time he mentioned registration. Mrs. Bard tried to pro-
ceed on the premise that here was a son whose father had

died in his absence. She told him of Pop's last days, how everyone at the ranch liked him, the final tragedy.

"Yeah, I heard the old man was ailing. I hadn't seen him for several years but I saw a fellow who said he wasn't doing so good."

That callous admission ended whatever sympathy she might have had for the son. Arrangements were rapidly concluded for going to Santa Barbara the next morning to straighten out Pop's estate, but for once Andy was not glad at the prospect of missing school. She trailed along when her mother took Mr. and Mrs. Reed to their cabin.

"This is where your father lived. There are all his things stacked in the corner."

"Humph! He didn't live very high, did he?"

"No, just this much higher than any help he got from you."

Reed seemed not to hear her sarcasm. His eyes probed the small pile of boxes that held Pop's things.

"The old man used to have a carved Chinese chest. What's happened to that? Did you take it?"

"No—he gave it to me the last time I saw him alive." Andy did not care whether or not Reed had intended to be so insulting. All that mattered was the threat to her last tie with Pop and Blue, the quaint little chest she cherished.

"He had no business to. I've always promised Dolores she could have it and I want it."

"Go and get it, dear."

"No!" Andy's sharp refusal surprised them all. Her mother's gentle pressure on her shoulder caused her to soften but not change her stand. "I'll give it to you tomorrow before you leave, but it's mine for one more night."

If Reed was going to insist, he changed his mind when Ross's tall figure loomed in the doorway. The couple was left alone when the others returned to the living room for their first private conclave since the younger Reed's arrival. Andy slumped in a chair, too dejected and brokenhearted for speech.

"I'll get a lawyer tomorrow, punkin. We'll show that pair of ghouls a thing or two," Ross promised her grimly.

"Thanks, Ross, but there's no use trying to fight it. We talked with the man from the courthouse before and he said that without something written by Pop my claim wouldn't stand up a minute. It's the papers or nothing. Just think how simple it'd be if those dudes could have been two minutes—one minute—later that day."

"You have their statements, Andrea. Maybe they would help a little."

"Not in a real contest, Mr. Hedges said. Well, I'm going to bed. There's one more chance to dream 'em up." Andy's smile was too thin to carry any conviction.

In her room she removed the chest's contents and, sitting cross-legged on the bed, holding it lovingly, she concentrated one last time on the paper's whereabouts. All she could think of, however, was Blue and how soon he would be leaving for good. Would his new owner—not Reed but the next one—treat the horse kindly?

Before long weariness overcame her. Not until the windows were gray with early morning light did she wake. That dream! She could still see how the envelope had

looked in the hollow live oak by the front porch right near where Pop had been sitting when she last talked with him. Andy started to jump up but the preceding day's exertions had stiffened her muscles like old leather. Nevertheless she hobbled about, flinging on the first clothes she found and in her stocking feet pattered outside.

She rushed straight to the hollow tree to peer in with the certainty of seeing the white rectangle so long sought for. The little rounded hollow was there all right but all it held was dead leaves and twigs and a few cobwebs. Andy couldn't hold back a sob. Still in her stocking feet she fled to the sanctuary of Blue's stall and his strong shoulder that soon glistened with her tears.

He bent his head around to nose her, cradling her with his curving neck and she felt comforted as she used to when her father's bear hug magically healed some childhood injury. Slowly the storm subsided as the sharpness of her grief receded, leaving one big all-over ache in its place.

"I'll spend what's left of the night with you, old fellow. This'll be our last time together."

Andy kicked some fresh bedding into a corner and sat down with her back to the partition. There Luis found her, slumped over in the corner, with Blue patiently standing guard when it was time for morning chores. There, hours later, she began her waking nightmare when they returned from town and the horse was legally Reed's. Ross's efforts and Andy's last minute pleading had been useless. The girl's only victory was in refusing to let Reed take Blue until after the trip to town when he had been declared the real owner.

For Keeps

Reed and his wife loaded their car without a hand being raised to help them. The entire Bar D contingent was there including Jump and Val who were awaiting sentence for deliberately missing their school bus and Jay who had made some bargain with his father for this extra crucial day. They all watched silently as Pop's possessions and the Chinese chest which Andy had not surrendered until the last minute were packed in the rear compartment.

"I hope he has a flat tire and has to take all that stuff out to get his spare," Andy muttered vindictively. "Oh, if only he would, or his car wouldn't start—anything to keep him here. I'm sure if I lose sight of Blue now I'll never see him again."

She had given up hoping by then and was praying for a miracle that would delay if not prevent Blue's departure. None was manifest. Reed banged the turtleback shut and turned toward the stable, the others following silently. He picked up Blue's halter but stood irresolutely by the stallion's stall, plainly hoping someone would go in to halter the horse for him.

"Go on in, Bert. He won't hurt you if a bunch of kids have been fooling with him," Mrs. Reed encouraged her husband, anxious to get away from that ring of hostile faces.

Affecting a jaunty air, the man slid the bolt, opened the door and sidled into the stall. Blue had been watching with interest but he was displeased when, instead of one of his friends, this distasteful stranger approached. The small ears flipped back and forth nervously as the stallion backed away.

"Whoa, Blue. Come here to me."

Blue paid no attention so Reed with a show of boldness went up to his head. After much fumbling with the halter he slipped it on the small head and fastened it. The spectators fell back in front of the man who led the stallion outdoors toward the trailer that for disreputable appearance and disrepair outdid Pop's which at least had been sound.

For one mad moment Andy thought of throwing herself into the trailer to prevent Blue's loading, for this was the end. He entered any trailer as quietly as his own stall and there could be no delay on that score yet her taut nerves cried, "Delay! Delay! Delay!"

"Hold it, man. You've got a flat tire there."

Ross's exclamation was as direct an answer to Andy's prayers as ever mortal could expect. She hurried around to the other side of the car and sure enough, the old tire with its worn spots was crumpled and creased by the rim that sat flush with the ground.

"Well, I'll be— That isn't just accident! It was all right a few minutes ago. If I lay my hands on the—"

"Watch it, fellow. I have ladies present whether you have or not." Ross's level tones brought Reed up short. "With a tire in that condition you needn't try to blame it on anyone. You're just lucky it didn't happen out on the highway or you might have had a bad smash."

The other did not appear convinced, however, and he glared around him silently. He seemed so positive it made Andy herself wonder, but they had all gone to the stable together. Jump was there too when Reed haltered the horse. Wasn't he? She turned and looked at her brother, his face so open and guileless, and though she saw no trace of guilt, the first smile in twenty-four hours quirked the corners of her mouth.

"Let me have Blue and I'll put him back in the stable for you while you change the tire."

This was the first offer of help, if it could be called that, and Reed suspiciously jerked the halter rope away from her outstretched hand.

"No, you don't! No telling what you'd do to him there out of sight. If you're gonna hold him, it'll be right here where I can watch you."

Andy had no pride when it was a question of her horse and she easily agreed to this insulting condition, but dangerous lights glimmered in the Bar D menfolks' eyes. Jay's fists clenched and unclenched nervously. Certainly any impulse to help the perspiring, jittery man was immediately forgotten so, still single-handed, he set about emptying the car's rear deck to get down to his tools and the spare. Soon it was as if he had never packed up. The ground was strewn with the familiar boxes and bags and the carved chest.

Even the latter had little power to affect Andy now that she had her beloved Blue for a few extra minutes. Everything and everyone else faded to shadows. Only she and the horse existed and to keep him real she relied on physical contact, a hand on his shoulder, a twist of mane between her fingers or she leaned her whole body against him as he moved around cropping the grass beside the driveway.

The hostility and tension were beginning to prey on Reed's rasped nerves. Twice he snarled at Andy to "Get back here!" Like one hypnotized into submission she obeyed, but she snapped awake when the last lug was tightened.

"Bring him here," he snapped. "I'll put him in now."

"Wouldn't it be better to load up the other things first? He'll have to spend enough hours in the trailer before he's through."

"I'll do it my way. He's *my* horse now. Gimme the rope."

Without a word Andy delivered Blue's lead shank into Reed's unsteady hand. With eyes red-rimmed and glassy from pent-up tears, she watched man and horse walk toward the trailer. Andy's thoughts contracted to pinpoint concentration as she flung a series of mental commands at the roan.

"Don't go in, Blue. Oh, don't go in. This time forget your manners."

Andy's scalp twitched, for her mind had barely formed the words before Blue pulled back so suddenly the man was nearly jerked off his feet. Reed's face flushed an angry red. He yanked the lead rope viciously. This threw the horse into rapid reverse, his backward rush carrying him many feet from the trailer, the silent semicircle giving ground accordingly.

There was something strange and wild in the horse's

behavior that Andy did not understand. There in full sunlight she shivered and her arms prickled with rising gooseflesh. Reed's patience lasted for one more try, when he too began to get rough. He threaded the rope over the soft blue nose. Each time the stallion pulled back the man jerked savagely on the rope. The struggle rapidly assumed the proportions of a royal fight, the red of distended nostril and whited eyes showing like battle flags on the blue horse.

"It's a strange trailer to him and there's something he's taken a dislike to. Just let him smell of it a minute and he'll probably walk right in." Sound horsemanship though it was Andy sensed insincerity in Jay's suggestion.

Puny humans might declare an armistice but not Blue. During the lull he stood spraddled, his front legs braced before him as he snorted blast after blast of defiance. He watched a rope being tied to the trailer side but he whirled first one way, then the other when Reed tried to pull it behind his back legs. Before this could be accomplished he had backed beyond the rope's length where he warily countered every move to lead him forward.

Reed's unstable temper exploded. He snatched up an old strap from the ground. Before anyone could stop him he lashed the stallion from head to heels with the buckle end. Until then Blue had merely resisted entering the trailer but now the man's anger was nothing compared to the stallion's towering fury.

He bellowed with rage and pain. Striking and kicking with cat-like quickness he seemed to have all four feet in the air at once. Reed held on to the lead rope—why, no one was ever able to explain afterward. It was long enough for

him to keep in the clear as Blue alternately plunged and
reared, swerving from one side of the trailer to the other.
One lunge knocked over Reed's pile of luggage and boxes
and scattered their contents around the yard.

The little chest stood naked and alone in the face of the
stallion's rage. Before Andy could spring forward to save
it, she was caught and held in Jay's muscular grip just as
the horse unleashed a mighty kick squarely against the
chest. It lofted into the air like a football, only to spatter
earthward in a shower of splinters and pieces.

Andy cried out with real anguish to see her cherished keepsake demolished. She rushed over to the debris to rescue what she could before it was trampled to nothing, but her cry of pain changed and swelled into a triumphant shout.

Blue's devastating one-two punch had done what Jay had suggested. No two pieces of the chest were left together and its secret bottom had no more secrets. There in full view of everyone was the long, white envelope of Andy's waking and sleeping dreams. Before her trembling fingers opened the flap to draw out two sheets of paper, one Blue's pedigree and registration, the other a handwritten will signed by Julius Reed bequeathing everything he owned including the stallion, Blue Smoke, to Andrea Bard, she knew that her search was ended. Blue was hers for keeps.

The horse himself, oblivious to the important shift his future had just taken, was giving Reed no quarter. Thought and action were simultaneous with Andy. She thrust the papers into Jay's hand before rushing headlong into the melee to snatch the rope away from Reed's limp fingers.

"Give me my horse. Whoa, Blue. Whoa! Easy, boy. Everything's going to be all right. Whoa, boy."

The horse recognized his friend's voice and steadied down momentarily, enabling Andy to turn him away from the hateful trailer. He willingly followed when she ran to the barn where she clapped him in his own stall. Then Andy dashed back to the others.

"You knew that chest had a secret bottom," she accused Reed, her voice trembling with anger and excitement. "No wonder you bullied it away from me. It's a good thing I didn't let you have it last night like you wanted or those papers would have been gone by now."

Meanwhile Ross and her mother had quickly glanced at the documents.

"*That* will stand up in any court in the United States," Ross declared, "and now there's nothing to keep you here longer. Pack up and get out!"

"I'll have the law on you for this. That horse is mine until the old man's will is recorded. I'll have you up for horse thievin'."

"Aw, go chase yourself." Any other time Muz would have challenged Andy's inelegant retort but it seemed to express her feelings as well.

"Let's be reasonable and talk this over." Pop's son adopted a different, more wheedling tone as he tried to salvage something from his fiasco. "How much were you willing to pay for the horse, Mr. Cameron?"

"He's worth several thousand dollars—and you know it," Ross retorted shortly, "but I won't give you a red cent now. He's not yours to sell. Now git!"

Reed shifted from one foot to the other, then shrugged. "Well, you can't blame me for trying."

The pair made short work of repacking, a simpler job now without Pop's belongings. A few minutes later car and trailer rattled out of sight.

"There! I hope that's the last we see of them," Andy said with satisfaction to Jay who had been standing beside her. Hearing no "Amen" she turned and saw him kneeling in the dirt, carefully gathering up the chest's fragments and putting them in a cardboard carton.

"There's a wonderful old cabinetmaker in Los Angeles, Andy, and maybe he can patch this together. Of course, it'll never be quite like it was but it's worth a try."

"Oh, yes, Jay. Under the circumstances I'm sure Pop wouldn't mind."

"It's strange that Pop would hide those papers in there without telling you anything about it. I wonder if he couldn't quite bring himself to trust us." Mrs. Bard voiced the question in everyone's mind.

"I don't think it was that, Muz. He was probably going to play a game with me, to see if I could figure it out. Now I can see that he left a clue I was too stupid to catch."

"Clue? Why didn't you tell me?" Jay exploded.

"It didn't seem important. It was that scrap of paper in the chest with all the horses' names on it."

"And—?"

"And he had underlined parts of two of them, 'Dark Secret' and 'Bottoms Up.' Plain as day now, eh?"

"Boy, was this put together neat," Jay exclaimed. "Look at that, would you—a false bottom that slips in there as snug as the real one."

"There's a tiny spring. Wonder where that came from? We've pushed and squeezed and pinched every inch of that chest without anything springing. Maybe it didn't work any more."

"No, we didn't," Jay cried after a pause. "See this leg. The spring fit in the top there. I'll bet if either of us had pressed hard on that leg, something'd have happened."

"'Clever these Chinee' for sure," Andy marveled. "That's too ingenious for me to ever figure out. Not a smart horse like Blue though. He worked it out at one crack you might say."

"But good," Jay agreed, carefully packing the last piece in the carton. "Come on, let's go and see how *your* horse is doing." He heavily accented the possessive pronoun.

That Blue still had the jitters they could tell the moment they entered the stable. He whirled to face them, his nostrils fluttering in and out at each strange sound. Andy and Jay showered the uneasy horse with attention to sooth his nerves. Andy dabbed lotion on a spot where Reed's brutal buckling had drawn blood.

"Jiminy, I sure agree with what Val said last night. I'm glad we had Ross here during this mess. I wish he could stay on instead of going back to New Mexico."

"*I* was here," Jay said stiffly. "You've got a crush on him and it's nauseating. He's old enough to be your father."

Andy's sudden, unaffected laughter was answer enough but she sobered before she made Jay feel ridiculous.

"Yes, he is old enough to be my father. I wish he were— since I can't have my own any more."

"I couldn't help hearing what you said." Ross's voice came from just outside the barn door. "Do you really mean it?"

This time it was not the horse but Andy and Jay who jumped with surprise and embarrassment.

"Yes, I do." Grave-faced and serious Andy turned to face an equally sober Cameron when he stepped through the doorway.

"What about Jump and Val?"

"They think so too. Val's already said so but Jump's the strong, silent type and would never admit it. He does though, I can tell by the way he tags you around. And he's always quoting you. It's 'Ross says' all day long."

"Well, that's a load off my mind. For a long time now I couldn't make up my mind whether I should propose to the mother or the children first. Now that I have your consent, I'll see what I can do." He turned to hurry away, calling back over his shoulder, "By the way, she sent me to call you to lunch—but you might take your time about it."

Andy, who could hardly bear to leave Blue for a second now that he belonged to her wholly and entirely, was glad of an excuse to linger with the stallion. To give Ross good measure they hailed Val and Jump with the news, thus keeping them away from the house.

"Of course, Reed has no one to blame but himself," Andy mused as the four relived the day's excitements. "If he hadn't been so piggish about the chest, or if he hadn't been so careless about his tires, or if he hadn't tried to get rough with Blue, all of it might never have happened. What I can't understand though is why Blue took such a violent dislike to that trailer," she puzzled. "It's not like him."

"Well—" Jay and Jump said in unison, only to look at each other with amazement.

"—you were so dead set on delays, Andy, any delays, I kind of saw to it that he had a flat tire," her brother admitted.

"—and while he was changing the tire, he and wifey were

so afraid you were going to pull a fast one with Blue, I rubbed a rag in that dead, that *very* dead cat down in the ravine," Jay confessed without an ounce of repentance, "and hid it in the trailer."

"Holy Toledo," Andy borrowed Ross's favorite exclamation. "No wonder Blue threw such a fit. You knew no one could force him in the trailer with that carrion smell."

Andy's last spark of resentment was extinguished with her burst of laughter that grew and swelled as the others joined her, their hilarity boiling higher and higher. It was just beginning to dwindle when Blue twitched his upper lip back in what looked like a horse laugh which sent the four youngsters into fresh spasms.

"What's so funny out here you can't hear the lunch bell?" Mrs. Bard demanded from the doorway where she and Ross were silhouetted. "If we don't eat pretty soon, we might as well call it supper."

"If we'd heard the bell, we'd have thought it was wedding bells. Dee dum dee dum," Andy hummed the wedding march as she seized Jay's and her brother's hands who in turn caught Val's until the four ringed their blushing elders with a merry circlet of congratulations.

When the laughter and excited exclamations had subsided Mrs. Bard repeated her entering question.

"Well, what was so funny? Us?"

"No, indeed," Andy disclaimed quickly before telling of the boys' shenanigans.

For an instant her mother tried to look shocked by these disclosures but soon her laughter joined Ross's booming baritone, sending the four young people into fresh seizure

Mrs. Bard was the first to regain some degree of composur

"They say 'all's fair in love and war' and this was both

She justified everything in one blanket statement. "Andy

in love with Blue and it was not only war, it was invasion